HAVE A NICE NIGHT

Lu Bradey is the best art-thief in the business, and a master of disguise, but his last job had fallen through. Now he's down on profits and needs to bring off something really big. He decides to take a trip to Paradise City—luxurious vacation resort of billionaires—and the perfect place for a massive jewel robbery.

Also by James Hadley Chase
CADE
GET A LOAD OF THIS
TRY THIS ONE FOR SIZE
YOU MUST BE KIDDING
and published by Corgi Books

James Hadley Chase

Have a Nice Night

CORGI BOOKS

HAVE A NICE NIGHT
A CORGI BOOK 0 552 12126 6

Originally published in Great Britain by Robert Hale Limited

PRINTING HISTORY
Robert Hale edition published 1982
Corgi edition published 1983
Corgi edition reprinted 1983
Corgi edition reissued 1990

This book is set in 10 pt. Caledonia

Corgi Books are published by Transworld Publishers
Ltd., 61–63 Uxbridge Road, Ealing, London W5 5SA, in
Australia by Transworld Publishers (Australia) Pty. Ltd.,
15–23 Helles Avenue, Moorebank, NSW 2170, and in New
Zealand by Transworld Publishers (N.Z.) Ltd., Cnr. Moselle
and Waipareira Avenues, Henderson, Auckland.

Printed and bound in Great Britain by
Cox & Wyman Ltd., Reading, Berks.

HAVE A NICE NIGHT

One

In a shabby, dimly lit bar on the waterfront of St. Johns River, Jacksonville, two men sat at a table and talked in low tones. Apart from these two and the fat, elderly barman, the bar was deserted.

The man sitting to the left was Ed Haddon: the king of art thieves: a brilliant operator who appeared to live an immaculate life of a wealthy retired business man, paying his taxes, moving to his various apartments in Fort Lauderdale, the South of France, Paris and London. He was the master mind who planned, organized and directed a group of expert thieves who profitably did his bidding.

Haddon could be mistaken for a senator or even a secretary of state. He was tall, heavily built, with thick iron-grey hair, a florid, handsome face and the benign smile of a politician. Behind this façade was a razor-sharp brain and a ruthless, cunning mind.

The man on the right was Lu Bradey: considered by the world's underworld as the best art thief in the business. He was slightly built, around thirty five years of age, with a black crewcut, sharp features and grey restless eyes. Apart from his expertise with any kind of lock, he was also a master of disguise. His facial skin was like rubber: a few pads inside his mouth and his lean face turned to fat. He made his own wigs. When he wore a moustache or a beard, each hair was put into place, one at the time. His thin body, by wearing padded clothes which he constructed himself, transformed him into a man whose main interest in life was heavy eating. Because of this remarkable talent for disguise, he had no police record, although the police of the world were searching for him.

These two men who had worked together for a number of years, had been holding a *post mortem* on their last job: the stealing of the Catherine the Great's icon from the Washington museum.* Both of them had agreed the planning had been brilliant and the execution of the steal not to be faulted. It was just one of those things that the planning, the organization and the thought hadn't paid off.

Taking his time, Haddon lit a cigar, and Bradey, recognizing the signs, waited expectantly.

'I lost money on that steal, Lu,' Haddon said when he was satisfied the cigar was drawing well. 'Okay, so it's so much water under the bridge. You lose one: you win one. Now, it's time we made a profit . . . right?'

Bradey nodded.

'You got something, Ed?'

'I wouldn't be sitting in this dump if I hadn't. This one will be big, but it needs working on. I will have to get together a good team.' He pointed his cigar at Bradey. 'You head my list. I need to know if you'll be available during the next three weeks.'

Bradey gave a sly smile.

'I'm always available when *you* want me, Ed.'

'Yeah.' Haddon nodded. 'I guess that's right. You know when I set up a deal, you make big money. Now, pay attention. When I was planning the icon steal, and because I had to work with that fag Claude Kendrick, I stayed for three days at the Spanish Bay Hotel, Paradise City. It cost me plenty. Now this hotel is very special. It is easily the most expensive and *de luxe* hotel in the world, and that's saying a lot. It doesn't have rooms, only suites.

* see *Try this one for size*.

It gives a service that is out of this world, and only people with more money than sense stay there, and let me tell you, Lu, there are still a lot of stupid jerks who *do* have more money than sense, so this hotel never, repeat never, has empty suites.'

Bradey lifted his eyebrows.

'You stayed there?'

'Correct. I move in the rich stream. That way, I pick up ideas. Okay, so it costs, but it often pays off. So this hotel has given me an idea.' Haddon puffed at his cigar, then flicked ash on the floor. 'The hotel is privately owned by a Frenchman, Jean Dulac, who knows his business. He is handsome, loads of charm and his rich clients adore him. His staff is hand-picked: some of them from France where the best food, the best hotel service and the hotel *de luxe* know-how comes from. I couldn't get a suite at the hotel. I stayed at one of a number of chalets in the grounds of the hotel: two bedrooms, living and so on: very *de luxe*. The suites are booked up all the year around. I was able to wander around the hotel. I had access to the lounges, the three restaurants, the swimming-pool.' He regarded Bradey. 'Very, very lush and stuffed with very, very rich men and women.'

Bradey was listening attentively.

'I don't need to tell you,' Haddon went on after a pause, 'that when men become rich, their wives want to compete with other rich men's wives. That's human nature. Apart from clothes, mink coats and so on, class jewellery comes high on the competitive list. If Mrs. Snook wears a diamond necklace, Mrs. Pook nags her husband until she gets one. Then Mrs. Snook adds ear-rings and bracelets to outdo Mrs. Pook who then demands ear-rings and bracelets. These spoilt bitches, who have never earned a dollar, demand and get gems worth thousands. Dinner at the hotel is the time to see these women in the main restaurant, plastered with diamonds, emeralds, rubies. I had dinner there, and I have never seen such a display of gems in one big room. I reckon on that particular night, these stupid, worthless women were wearing, between the lot of them, jewellery worth six or even seven million dollars.'

Bradey sighed.

'Very nice,' he said, 'So?'

'Yes.' Haddon puffed at his cigar. 'It occurred to me it would be a profitable idea to knock over the Spanish Bay Hotel.'

'Six million?' Bradey asked, staring at Haddon.

'Could be more, but let us say six.'

'Interesting.' Bradey scratched his head while he thought. 'I can't see it at the moment, Ed. Knock over the hotel? What does that mean exactly?'

'Of course you can't see it,' Haddon said and smiled. 'Smart as you are, Lu, you haven't my brains, that's why you and I work together so well. You organize the steal. I do the planning . . . right?'

Bradey nodded.

'So the take could be six,' he said, eyeing Haddon. 'What's in it for me?'

'Two,' Haddon said. 'I pay all the expenses. Fair enough?'

'Very nice,' Bradey said, 'and when we get the loot, who'll handle it?' Such was his faith in Haddon's planning, it didn't cross his mind to say *if* and not *when*.

'There'll be an uproar, of course,' Haddon said. 'The Paradise City cops are efficient. The squeal will come fast. They work well with the State Police and the Miami Police. It'll be too risky to try to get the stuff out of the city. I plan to dump the lot in Kendrick's lap. I'll have to talk to him, but he's our best bet.'

Bradey grimaced.

'I hate that fat fag.'

'Never mind. He's smart, and that's all we have to worry about.'

'Okay.' Bradey shrugged. 'What's this to be: a hold-up? I don't dig that, Ed: not a hotel. How's it going to be done?'

Haddon signalled to the fat barman to bring two more drinks. He waited until the barman brought the drinks and had removed the empty glasses.

'When I stayed at the hotel, Lu,' he said, after the two men had saluted and sipped their drink, 'I got talking to a fat old trout who was plastered with diamonds. You'll always find some old woman whose husband has been happy to die to be rid of her, sitting in hotel lounges. She was flattered I paid her attention. She told me she came to the hotel for a month every year. Every time she moved her fat body I could hear the rustle of dollar bills. I spent an hour with her, hearing about her husband, a big-shot in oil, who had died five years back, about her children and her goddamn grandchildren. She forced family photographs on me. You know the menace: catch the eye of a lonely old woman and you're in for a session. So, okay, I'm good at that. After a while, I admired her diamonds. At a guess, she had on around a hundred thousand worth. She told me she had always insisted her husband gave her for their wedding anniversaries, a present in diamonds. I asked her if she wasn't afraid that, in these days of snatch and grab, she would be robbed. She told me she would never wear the rocks outside the hotel. She said the security service given by the hotel was so good she never even thought of being robbed. We kept talking so I can tell you something about this security service. Every guest on arrival is given a security box with a scrambler lock. Only the guest knows the number of the scrambler. When the guests go to bed, they put all their valuables into the boxes and two security guards take the boxes to the hotel safe. Get the idea?'

Bradey nodded.

'Scrambler locks?' He smiled. 'No problem. Scrambler locks to me are chick feed.'

'I guessed you would say that. So when all these rich jerks go to bed, the hotel safe is stuffed with juicy boxes. That's as far as I have gone. Until the icon flop, I didn't

11

think of knocking over the hotel. Now, I'm sure it will pay off.'

Bradey thought, then asked, 'What's the hotel safe like?'

'That's for you to find out. I don't even know where it is located.'

'Okay. Shouldn't be difficult. Tell me about the security. Got any info about that?'

'There are two house dicks prowling around in shifts. Both look competent. Around nine p.m. two security guards, armed, come on duty and stay around until two a.m. They are young and tough. Life in the hotel quietens down around three a.m., but stray guests do come back after a night out up to four a.m. I think the best time to bust the safe would be around three a.m. I can't tell you more. You'll have to find out the details for yourself.'

'You mean for me to stay at the hotel?'

'No other way. I took the chance of you being available and got one of my people to book, through a travel agent, one of the hotel's chalets. That way the booking can't be traced.'

Bradey nodded approvingly.

'I've also paid a hefty deposit, so there'll be no problem. You move in next Monday under the name of Cornelius Vance.'

'Nice rich name.'

'I'll fix it for you to have a Rolls. Remember this is a very rich background you'll be moving into. I think you should be an old, very wealthy cripple in a wheel-chair with a male attendant. Don't get friendly with the other guests. Tell the hotel people you want to keep to yourself. This is going to cost me around fifteen thousand bucks, Lu. The chalet's rent without food, runs at eight hundred a day. Don't drink. Eat simply or the bill will reach the sky. Take your own drink with you. Have snacks in the chalet for lunch, but you have to eat in the restaurant at night to see the loot. Are you with me?'

Bradey nodded.

12

'Your job is to locate the safe and open it. We need a smooth operator who will drive the Rolls and mix with the staff. His job will be to locate the safe and help you shift the boxes when the time comes. That's the general plan. Now, pull it to pieces.'

'You say one of the house dicks is on duty at night?'

'Yes.'

'Two armed security guards are also around?'

'They won't worry you, Lu.' Haddon smiled. 'They were the first problem, plus the house dick, I knew I had to solve. This I have done. They won't bother you.'

'If you say so, Ed. Then let's take a look at my male attendant. I like the idea of me being in a wheel-chair. That way I'll be the last the cops will suspect until it's too late. I'll need a chauffeur to handle the boxes, but I don't dig him being my attendant. A pretty, sexy nurse will get more info than a guy. A pretty, sexy nurse in uniform can wander around the hotel, chat up everyone and get the general photo we need.'

'You are referring to your girl friend?' Haddon said.

'Yup. She's so sexy, I get a hard on even thinking about her. She's made to measure for this job.'

Haddon shrugged.

'I leave the details to you. I'll take care of the chauffeur. You take care of the nurse.'

'She comes under expenses, Ed?'

'My top for this job will be twenty grand and that includes everything.'

'Okay. Now, about the security guards and the house dick.'

Haddon finished his drink.

'Do you watch television?'

'I guess. Not often. To me, by and large, television stinks.'

'Ever watch the guy who captures wild animals?'

'Yeah. I've often thought they must lead a goddamn nice life: tough, but away from it all. So . . . ?'

'Seen a tiger put to sleep by a drugged dart?'

Bradey looked searchingly at Haddon.

'Yup.'

'Got me interested. I made inquiries through a good friend of mine.' Haddon reached down and picked up his briefcase and laid it on the table. He looked over at the barman who was busy reading a sporting sheet, looked around the deserted bar, then took from the briefcase what looked like a small air pistol. 'This cost me, Lu, but it works. It's loaded with six tiny darts loaded with the same knock-out mixture that the jungle guys use to knock out a tiger. The gun is automatic. All you have to do is to aim the gun at one of the guards, squeeze the trigger and he's asleep for at least six hours.'

Bradey gaped.

'I don't believe it.'

Haddon smiled.

'Come on, Lu. You should know by now I get things organized.'

'You mean you fire this gun and the guy hit goes to sleep?'

'That's it. Are you good with a gun, Lu?'

'Not me. I don't like guns. I've never carried a gun and never will.'

'I'll fix it for you to have a man who's a dead shot. He'll take care of the guards, drive the Rolls and help with handling the boxes. No problem.'

'You really mean this drug won't hurt anyone? No after-effects?'

'The guy goes to sleep, wakes up some six hours later and is fine.'

'Well, what do you know?' Bradey looked admiringly at Haddon. 'You certainly come up with ideas, Ed.'

'I guess. Now, you get your end organized. Suppose we meet at the Seaview Hotel, Miami on Saturday for lunch? I'll be staying there. We can then have a final run through. You'll check in at the Spanish Bay Hotel Monday afternoon. Okay?'

'Sure.'

'Right.' Haddon put the gun in his lap, concealing it by the table. He signalled to the barman. 'To set your mind at rest, Lu, I'll give you a demonstration.'

The fat barman came over and Haddon gave him a ten-dollar bill, telling him to keep the change. He watched the barman walk back to the bar, raised the gun, took aim and squeezed the trigger. There was a faint plopping sound. The barman started, clapped his hand to the back of his neck and turned to stare at Haddon who was closing his briefcase, then the barman's knees buckled and he spread out on the floor.

'Get the idea?' Haddon asked. 'Nice quick job, huh?'

Goggle-eyed, Bradey stared at the unconscious barman.

'Get the dart out of his neck, Lu,' Haddon said, 'and let's go.'

Getting unsteadily to his feet, Bradey crossed to the unconscious barman, located a tiny metal dart embedded in the barman's fat neck and withdrew it.

'You're sure he'll be all right?' he asked as he gave Haddon the dart.

'I'm sure. Come on, let's get out of here before someone comes in.'

The barman began to snore as the two men hurried out of the bar and into the hot, steamy sunshine.

* * *

Ever since the age of fourteen, Maggie Schultz had been a menace to men. Now, at the age of twenty-three, she was more deadly to men than a neutron bomb. She was beautiful in every possible way: blonde, her body so perfectly built all the glossy photographers, all the porn movie merchants fought for her services. She had climbed the ladder of whoredom, rung by rung, until she was now in the position to pick and choose. She had met Lu Bradey, and for the first time in her life, she had fallen in love. There were times when Bradey wondered what made this happen, knowing Maggie could have the pick of any man. He had explained to her that he was in the antique furniture business and was constantly travelling, but if she liked to move into his West-side apartment N.Y.C. and to continue her fashion modelling and to sleep with rich jerks who paid off, it was okay with him. Love was such a wonderful thing to Maggie, she agreed.

Maggie had been a help with the icon attempted steal. Bradey decided he must now put his cards on the table and bring her into his thieving fold. This could be tricky. Maggie was always happy to climb into any man's bed, but Bradey was a little doubtful if she would go along with thieving.

During the flight from Jacksonville to New York, he pondered the problem. He couldn't think of any girl who would play a sexy nurse as well as Maggie. He decided, because she was so madly in love with him, with the right approach, he could talk her into co-operating. Arriving at the airport, he went to a boutique and bought a giant cuddly panda. He knew Maggie, apart from mink and diamonds, was crazy about pandas.

He had already alerted her that he would be arriving. Her squeals of excitement and pleasure over the tele-phone line had nearly split his eardrum.

As he opened his apartment door, Maggie, stark naked, threw herself on him. For some seconds, he was nearly strangled. Then Maggie caught sight of the panda toy.

'Oh, look!' she cried. 'Oh, baby! Is it for me?'

'What do you think this place is . . . . a nudist club?' he asked, grinning.

She hugged the panda.

'Oh, darling! You're so wonderful! To think of this! I adore it! It's beautiful!'

Bradey set down his suitcase.

'Not as beautiful as you, honey. Let's have some action, huh?' and he went into the bedroom.

Half an hour later, Maggie was again cuddling the panda. Bradey, feeling spent, lay on his back, thinking there was no woman he had ever slept with who could drain him as Maggie did.

'Baby, how about a drink?' he asked.

'Of course.' She slid off the bed, still hugging the panda, and he watched her long beautiful back, her tight, rounded buttocks, her long, slim legs as she darted out of the room, and he sighed with content.

It wasn't until they had returned from dining at an exclusive and expensive restaurant and were seated side by side that Bradey began his sales talk.

'How would you like to stay a week in Paradise City?' he asked casually.

Maggie's china blue eyes opened wide.

'You mean that place where all the gorgeous billionaires live?'

'That's it.'

Maggie gave a squeal of delight and threw herself on Bradey who firmly pushed her away.

'Stop it, Maggie! Do you want to come with me?'

'Try and stop me! Paradise City! The things I've heard! Gorgeous hotels, palms, beaches, restaurants . . .'

'Cool it, Maggie. I'm going there to do a job. If you want to come, you'll have to help me.'

'Of course I'll help you, honey. I would do anything for you! You know that. I love you like crazy!'

'Maggie. Now listen. I'm not a dealer in antiques.'

Maggie giggled.

'I never thought you were, sweetheart. I was once in bed with an antique dealer. After he had huffed and puffed, he never stopped talking about what he sold and who to. His pad was stuffed with antiques.'

Bradey patted her hand.

'Smart girl.' He paused, then went on, 'I am a professional thief.' He waited for her reaction. She blinked, then nodded.

'You mean you steal from the rich and give to the poor? Like Robin Hood? I saw a re-run of Errol Flynn as Robin Hood. He was groovy.'

Bradey sighed.

'Never mind Flynn. I steal from the rich and put the proceeds in my pocket.'

Maggie considered this, then nodded.

'I always thought Robin Hood needed his head examined. Now, I'll tell you something, honey: there have been times when some rich old fink has been screwing me and when he went to sleep, I'd take a thousand or so from his wallet. So that makes me a thief too, doesn't it?'

Bradey sighed with relief. He was over the hurdle, now he had to instruct Maggie about what he wanted her to do.

He took her over Haddon's plan to rob the Spanish Bay Hotel. Maggie listened, and from her intent expression, Bradey was satisfied that she was absorbing what he told her.

'There's at least two million in it for us, baby,' he concluded. 'When I get the money, we'll get married.'

Maggie sighed.

'You said that the last time, but you didn't get any money and we aren't married. All I got was a trip to Switzerland and a diamond watch.' She kissed him gently. 'Don't think I'm moaning. I loved Switzerland and I adore my watch.'

'That job didn't jell,' Bradey said. 'This one will.'

'So what do I have to do?'

'I'm going to the hotel as an old man in a wheel-chair. You're going to be my nurse and companion. You will look a knock-out in a nurse's uniform.'

Maggie's face lit up.

'Oh, yes! I'd love that! I've always wanted to be a nurse! Honest, honey! I love helping rich old men. I really do! I mean it!'

Bradey contained his impatience with an effort. There were times when he found Maggie a trial.

'Your job is to find out where the safe is located. You will have to chat up the staff and sex the hotel dicks.'

Maggie clapped her hands.

'That'll be no problem.'

Looking at her, Bradey thought it would certainly not be a problem. Maggie could sex George Washington out of his grave.

'Well, baby, is it on?'

'Try and stop me!' Maggie cried and threw herself into his arms.

* * *

Having spent twenty years in various U.S. prisons, Art Bannion, now fifty years of age, had accepted the adage that crime doesn't pay.

Because of his association with many top criminals who had also been behind bars during his various incarcerations and becoming friendly with them, he had seen the opportunity of a new career which would help others and be profitable to himself.

With the aid of his wife, he was now established as possibly the only casting agency for the underworld. After all, he argued, in Hollywood they had casting agents to supply movie moguls with stars and bit-part players, so why not a casting agency to supply the right man or woman for a carefully planned crime? For the past five years he had built up his agency, drawing first on the names of those who had been in prison with him and had been released, then collecting names of those who were recommended as the up-and-coming younger criminal generation. All his business was done by telephone. He sat in a small office off Broadway N.Y.C. from 09.00 to 18.00, smoking, reading crime fiction and waiting for a call. His wife, Beth, sat in a smaller office, knitting sweaters which Art didn't want, but had pressed on him. When a call came, Beth would flick through the big card index with expert fingers and take the cards into Art's office and he would satisfy the client with the name and address of the man or woman who fitted the client's requirements.

Art took ten per cent of whatever the man or woman he supplied was paid. This was a satisfactory arrangement for both the client and Art, and during the years, Art made a considerable amount of money, always in cash, and free from the grasping claws of the IRS. His activities were hidden behind a plaque on the door that read: *The World-wide Bible Reading Society*. He was bothered neither by visitors nor the police.

This morning, Art Bannion, lean, balding, and with features a buzzard might envy, lolled in his desk chair, his feet on the desk, contemplating his past life. From time to time when he was bored reading crime fiction and when the telephone remained silent, he would think of his mistakes and his life in various prisons, and even of his mother and father.

His parents had been small-time farmers who were happy to slave on the land and earn, to Art's thinking, pea-nuts. His brother, Mike, ten years younger than Art hadn't had Art's driving ambition. Art had left home when he was seventeen, thirsting for money and the bright lights. After a year of semi-starvation in New York, he was caught with two other men, trying to bust a bank safe. He went to prison for two years. From then on, he never stopped trying for the fast buck, and did so badly, he was continually being picked up and thrown in the slammer. When his parents died, his brother, Mike, joined the regular army and worked his way up to Musketry Sergeant which Art considered to be one of the lowest forms of animal life. However, he was fond of his brother who never interfered, never criticized, always visited him when he was in prison and never attempted to change Art's way of life. There was a strong bond between the two men, and Art had a sneaking admiration for his brother which he kept to himself.

When Art finally accepted the fact that crime didn't pay, he looked around, found and wedded Beth, a small, fat, easy-going woman of forty whose father was serving life for murder and whose mother ran a sleazy brothel in

New Orleans. Beth was happy to help Art run his crime-casting agency and to have a well-furnished, comfortable four-room apartment.

Sitting at his desk, thinking about his past, Art turned his thoughts to his brother, and his face saddened. Mike had had a real tough break: a break that Art wouldn't wish on his worst enemy. When Mike had reached the rank of sergeant, he had married. Art had only met Mike's wife, Mary, once, but he had approved. She was a nice, attractive girl who made Mike more than happy. Mike broke the news of his wedding when visiting Art, in prison, some six years ago. With a beaming smile, he had told Art that he and Mary were planning on a big family. Art forced himself to look pleased, but he thought anyone wanting children should have his head examined. Mike had been transferred to California, and the brothers had lost touch for some years. Art had vaguely wondered how Mike was getting on, but he was no letter writer, and he was fully occupied building up his agency.

Now, two weeks ago, he had had a telephone call from Mike asking if they could meet. There was a note in Mike's voice that alerted Art that something was wrong. He had told Mike to come to his apartment, but Mike had said he wanted to talk to Art alone.

'That's no problem,' Art had said. 'Beth can go see a friend. Something up?'

'That's what I want to talk to you about,' Mike had said. 'See you then at your place at seven tonight,' and he had hung up.

Thinking back on the meeting, Art grimaced. When he had opened the front door of his apartment in answer to the ring on the bell, he was confronted by a man he scarcely recognized as his brother. The last time he had seen Mike he had envied his physique and that look the Army gives to its regulars. Mike was a shadow of his old self: thin, his face drawn, his eyes sunken and despair exuding from him that Art could almost feel.

The two men had sat down in the quiet of Art's

21

living-room and Art had listened. Mike had sketched those six years the brothers hadn't met in short curt sentences.

A year after his marriage, a baby girl arrived: a mongol. Mary had given up her job to be with the baby, named Chrissy, and tended her with loving care. They had to reduce their standards of living and make do on Mike's Army pay.

'Jesus!' Art had exclaimed. 'I'm sorry. Mongol baby? What the hell's that?'

'A mentally retarded child,' Mike had told him. 'A darling, affectionate kid who will never learn to write and only talk with difficulty. Never mind. It was our burden, and we were both crazy about her.'

'So . . . ?'

Mike stared into space for a long moment and the despair that sat with him deepened.

'Mary was killed by a hit-and-run three weeks ago.'

Art sat forward, staring at his brother.

'You mean your wife got killed?' he jerked out.

'Yes.'

'For God's sake, Mike! Why didn't you tell me?'

Mike shrugged.

'I'm telling you now.'

'But why *now*? I could have done something. I could have been with you. For God's sake . . .'

'No one could have done anything for me,' Mike said quietly. 'I had to sort it out for myself. Now, I have no wife and Chrissy on my hands. I've put her in a home near my barracks so I can see her weekends. I got rid of my little house. I now live in barracks. This home is good for Chrissy, but it costs. I've managed so far.'

'You want money, Mike? I can give you some. How much do you want? I'll do what I can.'

'Not the kind of money I need, Art,' Mike said.

'What's that mean?' Art asked. 'I could lend you a couple of grand. Damn it! I can give you the money.'

'I need at least fifty thousand,' Mike said.

Art gaped at him.

'You crazy? What the hell do you want all that money for?'

'It's to take care of Chrissy. I've talked to the doctor who runs the home. He's a good guy. He tells me Chrissy has a malformation of her heart. It's the usual thing with mongols. She won't live for more than fifteen years. To give her the best attention, and I know she would get the best attention at this home, it's going to cost fifty thousand dollars, and that will take care of her for the rest of her short life.'

'But Mike! You're earning! I'll chip in. You don't have to find all this money at once. You can pay the home month by month.'

Mike nodded.

'That's what I thought, but I'll be dead in another five or six months.'

Art stiffened. Looking at his brother, seeing the thin face and the sunken eyes, he felt a chill crawl up his spine.

'Dead? Don't talk crap! You're good for twenty years! What are you talking about?'

Mike stared at the whisky in his glass for a long moment, then looked straight at his brother.

'I have a terminal cancer,' he said quietly.

Art closed his eyes. He felt the blood drain out of his face.

There was a long silence, then Mike said, 'For the past two years, I have had odd pains. They come and they go. I didn't tell Mary. I thought it was nothing. You know? People have pains, and it is nothing, but they make a fuss. When I lost Mary, and these pains got worse, I got worried about Chrissy, so I talked to the M.O. He fixed for me to see a specialist at Northport, Long Island. That's why I'm here. I saw him a couple of days ago and he told me I had around six months to live. I'll have to go into hospital in a couple of months, and I won't be coming out.'

'God! I'm sorry!' Art said. 'This quack could be wrong.'

'He isn't. Now, forget it. Let's talk business, Art.' Mike looked straight at his brother. 'You told me what your racket is: finding men to pull a crime. There is no way I can raise fifty thousand dollars, but I've got to do just that. I don't care what I do as I have only a few months to live. Can you get me a job that'll pay fifty grand? For Chrissy, I'll even go to murder. What can you do?'

Art took out his handkerchief and mopped his sweating face.

'I don't know, Mike. I see your reasoning, but fifty grand for a job is pretty scarce. You're an amateur. You have no police record. My people wouldn't want to work with you. A job that pays that big is kept in the family so to speak.'

'Skip that, Art,' Mike said, a grating note in his voice. 'I'm relying on you. Whatever the job is, I'll do it, and I'll do it well. I have a month's sick leave. I'll stay here until you find something. I'm at the Mirador Hotel.' He got to his feet. 'Anything—repeat anything—that pays fifty grand. Think about it, Art. I'm relying on you. Okay?'

Art nodded.

'I'll do what I can, but I can't promise anything.'

Mike stared at him.

'I'm relying on you,' he said. 'In your bad days, I stayed with you. Now, I expect you to stay with me. So long for now,' and he left.

Art had done his best, but his regulars would have nothing to do with an amateur, and this morning, he sat at his desk, at his wits' end to find a job that would pay his brother fifty thousand dollars. He wondered if he should sell stock, but he knew Beth wouldn't stand for that. He had discussed the situation with her and she had been unsympathetic. 'Dotty brats should be smothered at birth,' she had said. 'One thing you don't do, Art, you don't sell stock and give our money to Mike. Is that understood?'

A week had passed since his brother's visit. Art had

24

heard nothing from him, but the memory of those sunken eyes and the look of despair haunted him.

Interrupting his dismal thoughts, Beth put her head around his office door.

'Ed Haddon on the line, Art,' she said.

Art stiffened to attention. Haddon was his most profitable client. He had supplied Haddon with many top-class thieves, and Haddon paid generously.

Picking up the receiver, he said, 'Hi, Mr. Haddon! Good to hear from you. Something I can do?'

'I wouldn't be telephoning just to hear your voice,' Haddon snapped. 'I want a man: good appearance, a dead shot, able to handle a Rolls Royce and act the part of a chauffeur.'

Art drew in a long deep breath. This looked custom-made for Mike.

'No problem, Mr. Haddon. I've got just the man. What's the job?'

'A big one. It'll pay around sixty thousand.'

Art closed his eyes. This was too good to be true.

'No problem, Mr. Haddon.'

'Who's your man?'

'My brother. He's a top-class shot and needs the money. You can rely on him.'

'What's his police record look like?'

'He hasn't one, Mr. Haddon. Right now he is a Musketry instructor in the Army. He looks good, talks well and is a certain shot.' So anxious was Art to get his brother fixed, he went on, 'I will guarantee him, Mr. Haddon.' The moment he had said this, he regretted it. How did he know that Mike would deliver to Haddon's satisfaction? Haddon was ruthless. So far, Art had given him more than satisfaction, but he knew for sure, one slip and Haddon would deal with him no longer. Haddon's account with Art was the guts of his agency. If Haddon dropped him, so would all his other clients drop him. He broke out into a cold sweat, but he had shot off his mouth, and there was no retreat.

Haddon said, 'That's fine with me. If you guarantee your brother, that's good enough for me. Okay, tell him to report to Cornelius Vance at the Seaview Hotel, Miami at ten o'clock Sunday twenty-third.'

'How about the gun?'

'Vance will give him that, and Bannion, there is no violence. No one gets killed, but this man has to be a dead shot.'

'When's the pay-off, Mr. Haddon?'

'When the job's done. It'll take around a couple of months. This is a big one, Bannion. You screw it up, and you'll be out of business,' and Haddon hung up.

Beth stormed into the office.

'I was listening,' she said, her face cherry red. 'You gone out of your mind? That pin-head of a soldier? We have dozens of dead shots on the cards. Why pick on him . . . a goddamn amateur?'

Art glared at her.

'He's my brother. He needs help. Go away!'

When Beth, grumbling, had gone, Art dialled the Mirador Hotel number and asked to speak to Mr. Mike Bannion. He expected his brother would be out on this mild sunny morning, but Mike came on the line immediately.

Art thought: The poor bastard has been sitting in his dreary hotel room, waiting for me to call. Well, I've good news for him.

When Art had told him the news, Mike said with a catch in his voice, 'I knew I could rely on you, Art, more than thanks. I won't let you down. I'll get going right away, but I need money.'

'That's okay, Mike. I'll send you three thousand in cash to your hotel. Don't skimp on the chauffeur's uniform. It has to be convincing. My client is important.'

There was a long pause, then Mike said, 'No one gets killed?'

'That's what the man said.'

26

'Okay, Art, and thanks again. You can rely on me,' and Mike hung up.

Art sat back in his chair wondering if he should consider himself a saint or a sucker.

Two

Anita Certes entered the second bathroom of the penthouse suite of the Spanish Bay Hotel, bracing herself for what she knew she would find.

The penthouse suite, the most luxurious and most expensive suite in the hotel had been taken by Wilbur Warrenton, the son of Silas Warrenton, a Texas oil billionaire. Just married to Maria Gomey, a South American, whose father owned a number of silver mines, Wilbur had decided that Paradise City would be the place to spend their honeymoon, and Maria, difficult to please, had agreed.

At the age of twenty-nine, Wilbur had not, as yet, joined the Texas Oil Corporation over which his father reigned. He had had a Harvard education, taking a Master's degree in economics, had spent a year in the Army as Major (Tanks), had travelled the world in one of his father's yachts, had met Maria, fallen in love and married. When the honeymoon ended, he was to become one of the ten vice-presidents of his father's vast oil kingdom.

His father, Silas Warrenton, a tough oil-man, had no love for anyone except his son. Silas's wife had died a few years after Wilbur's birth, and Silas, who had been deeply in love, had transferred this love to his son. When Wilbur told his father that he wanted to marry and had introduced Maria, Silas had stared thoughtfully at her. Her dark complexion, her slim, sensual body, her big sexy eyes and her hard mouth gave him doubts, but he knew of her father with his billions, so he mentally shrugged. If this piece was what his son wanted to marry, he would raise no objection. After all, he told himself, she was worth screwing and divorce was easy. So he gave her a crooked smile, patted her shoulder and said, 'I want grandchildren, my dear. Don't disappoint me.'

Maria thought he was the most horrible, vulgar old man alive. Even when Wilbur had hinted he too would like children, she had stared bleakly at him.

'Later. Let's be happy and free while we are young. Children always bring trouble.'

Anita Certes was one of the many bedroom maids employed by the Spanish Bay Hotel. At the age of twenty-three, she was squatly built, dark-complexioned, hair like a raven's wing and a Cuban. She had been working at the hotel for the past twelve months. Her job was to clean the bathrooms, change the bed linen daily, dust and clean.

Anita had 'done' Wilbur's bathroom. That was no problem. He even folded his bath towels, and there was no mess, but Maria's bathroom made Anita boil with suppressed fury.

What a goddamn slut this rich, spoilt woman was! Anita thought as she surveyed the mess she was now faced with to clear up.

Sodden towels lay on the floor. (Did she take the towels into the bath with her? Anita wondered.) Face powder and eyelash black splattered the mirrors. A trodden lipstick smeared the floor tiles. The toilet hadn't been flushed.

The rich! Anita thought as she gathered up the sodden towels. Even if she was worth millions as this bitch was, she would never dream of leaving a bathroom in this disgusting state.

As she worked, her mind shifted to her husband, Pedro. They had been married for two years. They had come, on Pedro's urging, to Florida in the hope of bettering their economic condition which had been hard in Havana. Anita had been lucky to have got the cleaning job at the Spanish Bay Hotel, but Pedro could find only occasional work, street cleaning, which paid little.

To her, Pedro was the most handsome man alive. She loved him fiercely and possessively: adoring this slim, dark man, accepting his bad tempers, his constant complaints, giving him everything she earned. They lived in a one-room walk-up in Seacomb which was on the outskirts of Paradise City and where the workers lived. She was so in love with Pedro it didn't occur to her that he was a wastrel. After a few days with a brush and cart, street cleaning, he had given up. His one thought was to return to his father's small sugar cane farm although a year ago his one thought was to leave it. Anita, listening to his complaints, had kissed him, telling him to be patient. Something good for him would turn up. Cutting sugar cane was no way to live. She would work harder and she would provide. Pedro had smiled. Okay, so they would wait.

While she worked, clearing up the mess in the bathroom, she wondered what Pedro was doing. He told her he would be walking the streets, trying to find a job, but she wondered. At the end of each week, he had spent all the money she had earned. Often, there wasn't money enough to buy more rice, and he had complained. Anita, adoring him, promised to work harder.

While she worked, making Maria Warrenton's bathroom immaculate, Pedro Certes was sitting in a shabby bar in Seacomb. With him was Roberto Fuentes. Both men were drinking beer.

Fuentes a Cuban, had lived in Seacomb for the past three years. A short, over-fat man with glittering hard eyes, he had carved out a small living on the waterfront, cleaning and helping to service the many yachts of the rich.

He liked Pedro and listened to Pedro's constant complaints. This evening, he had decided that Pedro was ripe for a job that could make Fuentes some three thousand dollars. Fuentes believed that risks were not for him. If a man could pick up some three thousand dollars and find someone to take the risk, the idea was worth considering.

Speaking in a low voice, he said, 'Pedro. How would you like to pick up a thousand dollars?'

Pedro twiddled his glass of warming beer, then looked at Fuentes.

'Why talk this way? A thousand dollars? With that money I could take my wife and myself back to my father's farm. What are you saying?'

Fuentes smiled. His smile was like the flickering tongue of a snake.

'It can be arranged. It depends on you. A thousand dollars! Nice, huh?'

Pedro nodded.

'More than nice. Keep talking.'

'You know where my room is on Coral Street? The big block of walk-ups?'

'I know it.'

'There are seventy tenants in this block. Each of them pay sixty dollars a week rent. That makes a take of forty-two hundred dollars. Right?'

'So what?' Pedro asked.

'You and I could grab that dough. To you, it'll be as easy as screwing your wife.'

Pedro's eyes narrowed. A thousand easy dollars!

'Keep talking,' he said. 'You've got me interested.'

'Living in this block is Abe Levi. He works for the people who own the block. He's their rent collector as well as the janitor. Every Friday he goes from flat to flat and collects the rent money: forty-two hundred dollars. He goes back to his flat, writes the amounts up, then the following morning takes the money to the rental office. He's been doing this for years. I've watched him. Now Levi is a creep without spine. If you waved a gun in his face, he would faint. He is fat and old. All we have to do is to walk in while he's counting the dough, wave a gun in his face and we have got forty-two hundred dollars. I tell you, Pedro, it's as easy and simple as that.'

Pedro's eyes sparkled.

'I like it,' he said, 'So tomorrow?'

'Yes.' Fuentes gave his snake's smile. 'But you have to handle Levi. If I walked in, he would recognize me, but you, waving the gun, he wouldn't know. I stay outside, you do the business . . . right?'

Pedro's eyes lost their sparkle. He thought, then shook his head.

'So you don't take a risk, but I do . . . right?'

'There is no risk.' Fuentes leaned forward and patted Pedro's arm. 'You walk in, wave the gun, Levi faints, you collect the money, and we're both happy.'

'For this, I want two thousand,' Pedro said firmly.

Fuentes grimaced.

'Because we are friends, I am offering you the chance to make money. I can get anyone to do this job. It's so easy. No. Two thousand is out.'

'Fifteen hundred or you find someone else.'

Fuentes hesitated, then gave his snake's smile.

'Agreed.' He leaned forward. 'Let's talk about it.'

When Anita climbed the five flights of stairs and entered her one-room home, she found Pedro lying on the bed, a cigarette dangling from his lips and a contented smile on his face.

Anita was off-duty until 20.00 when she returned to the hotel to once again clean the penthouse suite. The time now was 17.00, and she was feeling tired and depressed, but seeing Pedro so relaxed, she brightened.

'You have found a job!' she exclaimed. 'I can see it on your face!'

'Saturday we return to Havana,' Pedro said. 'I'll have the money for the flight, and enough for us to help my father.'

Anita stared at him.

'But that is not possible!'

'It is.' He put his hand under the pillow and produced the .38 revolver Fuentes had given him. 'With this, anything is possible.'

Anita sat down abruptly, feeling faint. For sometime now, she suspected that Pedro would be driven to do something desperate.

'Darling, please! You mustn't!'

Pedro pushed the gun under the pillow.

'I have had enough.' His thin face turned vicious. 'I must have money to return home. Fuentes and I have discussed this. There is no risk. Saturday, I go. If you want to stay, then stay. I'm going home with fifteen hundred dollars. That is final.'

'There is always a risk,' Anita said, her voice trembling.

'Not this time. Saturday we leave. Now get me something to eat.'

Anita had made friends with the third chef at the Spanish Bay Hotel. She allowed him, from time to time, to put his hand up her skirt for a gentle feel, and, in return, he gave her leftovers: bits of good steak, bits of chicken and sometimes even a slice of fruit tart. As she sat, staring at Pedro, she nursed the plastic sack the chef had given her, and Pedro was looking hungrily at the sack. He hadn't eaten all day.

'You really mean you are going to steal, my darling?' she asked.

'You heard! Get me something to eat!'

She got slowly to her feet and walked unsteadily into the tiny kitchen.

* * *

Detective 1st Grade Tom Lepski liked Fridays. Unless there was some emergency, and in Paradise City, this was rare, he could sign off and return home for the week-end. Okay, there was Carroll, his wife, to nag him to do household chores and cut the lawn, but he was away from the detectives' room and even household chores were minor to sitting around waiting for crime.

He looked at his watch. Another ten minutes, and he would be off. Carroll had told him there would be a chicken and ham pie for dinner. Lepski liked his food, and chicken and ham pie was one of his special favourites.

Max Jacoby, 2nd Grade detective, was thumping out a stolen car report. He and Lepski worked well together.

'Chicken and ham pie!' Lepski exclaimed. 'Man! I dig that pie!'

Jacoby paused in his typing.

'There are times when I envy you, Tom,' he said. 'To be married to a great girl like Carroll! When I sign off, I'll be going to Fung-U for a take-home dinner . . . ugh!'

Lepski looked smug.

'It's time you got married, Max. That junk food is not for me. Carroll would flip her lid to think of me eating that kind of swill.'

'I guess.' Jacoby sighed and resumed his typing.

The telephone on Lepski's desk came alive. He snatched up the receiver and bellowed. 'Detective Lepski! What do you want?'

'Lepski! Do you have to be so common and shout like that?'

Lepski groaned, recognizing his wife's voice.

'Oh, it's you, honey,' he said, lowering his voice.

'Yes, it's me,' Carroll said. 'Really, Tom, you should try to be more refined when answering the telephone.'

'Okay.' Lepski loosened his tie. 'I'll be home in twenty minutes. How's the pie looking?'

'That's why I'm calling. I had Mavis here. She was telling me about her husband. Really, Tom, the way that man behaves! I just sat listening, speechless.'

Lepski shifted restlessly in his chair.

'Okay, feed me the details when I get home. How's the pie looking?'

There was a pause, then Carroll said, 'A little trouble. When Mavis was telling me about Joe, I sort of forgot the pie was in the oven. The things that man does to her! You can't believe it! I was absolutely speechless!'

Lepski began to drum his fingers on his desk.

'You forgot the goddamn pie was in the oven?'

'Don't swear, Lepski. It's vulgar.'

Lepski picked up a pencil and snapped it in two. Jacoby stopped typing and sat back to listen.

'What's happened to the pie?' Lepski bawled.

'I wish you wouldn't shout. I'm calling to tell you to stop off at Fung-U's take-home shop and bring us something to eat,' Carroll said. 'Otherwise, we'll have nothing,' and she hung up.

Lepski slammed down the receiver and glared at Jacoby who quickly resumed his typing. Snorting, Lepski stormed out of the detectives' room.

As he reached the charge room, about to sign off, Sergeant Joe Beigler appeared.

Beigler, a big, fleshy, freckle-faced man, was in charge of headquarters while Chief of Police Fred Terrell was absent.

'I have a job for you, Tom,' he said.

Lepski glared at him.

'I'm signing off!'

'You'll love this one, Tom. I could give it to Max, but I've decided you were the boy.'

'Give it to Max. I've got to buy dinner! Carroll's burned my goddamn chicken and ham pie!'

'If I gave it to Max, you'd never forgive me,' Beigler said, grinning.

'So what's the goddamn job?' Lepski demanded, getting interested.

'A complaint has just come in about the G-String Club,' Beigler said. 'A Mrs. Abrahams took her husband there last night. She says the girls there weren't wearing their G-strings.'

Lepski's eyes popped wide open.

'You mean they were going around starkers?'

'That's what Mrs. Abrahams says. Can't have that, Tom.

You'd better talk to Harry. If the mayor gets to hear of this, he'll slam the club shut.'

'Wouldn't want that to happen,' Lepski said.

'Just warn him, huh?'

'You bet. No G-strings? What's one old bag's poison, is another man's meat,' Lepski said, his eyes glistening. 'Do me a favour, Joe. Call Carroll. Tell her I won't be home. Tell her I'm on a smash and grab.'

'Leave it to me,' Beigler said, knowing Carroll. 'I'll make out you're being a hero.'

'Don't overdo it, Joe. Carroll is tricky. Just say I've been called out on a smash and grab. Right?'

'Leave it to me, Tom.'

Harry Atkin, the owner of the G-string Club, was a good friend of the police. His club, situated on a side street off Seacomb's main street was well patronized. When the rich felt in the mood to slum, they spent most of the night at the club, eating excellent sea food, served by gorgeous girls who were topless and with G-strings. His was a thriving business.

From time to time, when Lepski was in the district, he would drop in and shoot the breeze with Harry, have a couple of free drinks, admire the girls then go about his business. This was something he didn't mention to Carroll, knowing she wouldn't approve.

Around 19.45, he arrived at the club, walked down the stairs into the big room where three blacks were polishing and cleaning, ready for the night's entertainment.

Harry Atkin, a short, fat man with fiery red hair, was behind the bar, reading the evening paper. He looked up and his smile was wide when he saw Lepski.

'Hi, Tom! Haven't seen you in weeks. How are they hanging?'

Lepski climbed onto a stool, shook Harry's hand and pushed his hat to the back of his head.

'Fine,' he said 'And you?'

'Couldn't be better. There's going to be a big crowd here tonight. Had a big crowd last night.' He reached for a bottle of Cutty Sark, knowing this was Lepski's favourite tipple, and poured a big drink, added ice and pushed the glass across the counter.

'Harry,' Lepski said, after a long pull at the drink, 'There's been a complaint.'

Harry nodded.

'I was waiting for it, Tom. Just one of those things. That old bag, Mrs. Abrahams, huh?'

'That's the one. What's going on, Harry? She complains the chicks weren't wearing their G-strings.' Lepski leered. 'I'd like to have been there, but you can't do that sort of thing. It'll get you a bad name.'

'She's lying. I'll tell you what happened. We had a couple of rich drunks, sitting at an adjacent table where this old bag was, plus her creep of a husband. Lu-Lu was serving fish soup, and she was bending over with her arse in the air.'

Lepski who had seen Lu-Lu and thought she had the sexiest bottom of all the girls in the club, nodded.

'So one of the drunks snipped Lu-Lu's G-string and the goddamn thing fell into the old bag's soup!' Harry burst out laughing. 'It was the damnedest thing, with the old bag having hysterics, her husband getting a hard on for the first time in years, and Lu-Lu clutching her pussy. The two drunks had a real ball. In fact, everyone in the joint loved it, except the old bag.'

Also laughing, Lepski mopped his eyes.

'I love it! I'd give my right arm to have been there.'

'Yeah. I got Lu-Lu out of sight, tried to pour oil on the old bag, but she grabbed her husband and left, shouting she was going to complain to the mayor.'

'Okay, Harry, relax. I'll put in a report. Don't worry your brains. When I tell the boys back at headquarters, they'll split their sides. No other girl lost her G-string?'

'I'll have you know, Tom, my girls are respectable,' Harry said, looking serious. 'The last thing they are going to lose is their G-strings.'

Lepski laughed.

'For God's sake, Harry, what else have they to lose?' He finished his drink, looked at his watch, saw it was now after 20.00, and remembered he had to buy dinner. 'Do me a favour, Harry. Carroll has burned the pie we were going to have. How about one of your pizzas?'

'Wouldn't think of it. For you, Tom, I'll fix a real meal. How about chicken in mushroom and white wine sauce? All your good lady will have to do is to put it in the oven for twenty minutes.'

Lepski's eyes glistened.

'Sounds great.'

'Okay. Help yourself to another drink. I'll fix it with Charlie.'

As Harry hurried off, Lepski reached for the bottle of Cutty Sark. There were times when police work paid off, he thought. A cool hand took him by the wrist.

'Let me do that for you, Mr. Lepski.'

Looking up, Lepski was confronted by a pair of small breasts with shell-pink nipples and found a girl wearing only a G-string and black, high-heeled shoes, smiling at him.

'I'm Marian,' the girl said, fluttering long eye lashes. 'You heard about Lu-Lu? Wasn't that terrible?'

Lepski opened and shut his mouth, but no words came. His eyes feasted on this gorgeous little body right by his side.

Smiling, Marian poured the drink, added ice and placed the glass in his hand.

'Mr. Lepski,' she said, sitting on a high stool by his side. 'I think, and so do all the girls, you are the most handsome cop in the City. You know?'

Lepski beamed. Police work! he thought. Who wouldn't be a cop?

* * *

Across the narrow street, opposite the G-String Club was a highrise of one or two-room apartments, strictly for the workers.

Abe Levi hated Fridays. This rent-collecting drag was slowly killing him. There was always some whining excuse not to pay, and he always had to turn tough which was against his nature. The Syndicate who owned the highrise had told him there was to be no credit. If the jerks couldn't find the rent, out they went. It hurt Abe to deliver the message. He wanted to be on good terms with the tenants, but threatening them made this impossible.

'Look,' he would say, 'don't blame me. Pay or you're out. That's what the boss says. It's nothing to do with me.'

Squeezing the rent from so many tenants took time, and when he had visited the last apartment, collected the rent with a struggle, it was well after 20.00. He was anxious to return to his ground-floor two-room apartment and have supper.

Abe Levi was a thick-set Jew with a mop of grey hair and a bushy beard. Life hadn't been easy for him. When young, he had helped his father sell fruit from a barrow. Later, he had married a girl who had slaved in a clothing factory. When his parents died, he had given up the fruit barrow. A friend had got him this rent-collecting job. It was a lot better than tramping the streets, pushing a heavy barrow. His wife had died two years ago. There were no children. Abe spent his lonely nights watching television, and once a week, he went to the Jewish club where he was always welcomed.

As he got into the elevator, he thought sadly of his wife, Hannah. She always had a hot meal waiting for him. This night, he would eat a bit of soused fish, but there would be a good TV serial on which he was following.

Carrying the heavy rent bag, now stuffed with bills and coins, he left the elevator and walked down the long dark passage to his front door. Two of the passage lights were out. This, he would have to fix, he thought wearily before he ate. It was his responsibility to keep the highrise in order.

Reaching his apartment door, he fumbled with his key, unlocked the door and entered his living-room. His hand groped for the light switch, pressed it, but he remained in darkness. He groaned to himself. A goddamn fuse had blown! That meant a trip down to the basement.

Abe was a careful man. He was always prepared for an emergency. He kept a powerful flashlight on a small table just inside his living-room. As he groped for it, he received a violent shove between his shoulder blades that sent him staggering into the darkness. His thighs hit the arm of his TV chair and he toppled and went sprawling, but even falling so heavily, he held onto the rent bag.

Pedro Certes, breathing fast, his heart pounding, had been waiting. He had unscrewed a lamp in the passage, put a bit of tin foil around the end of the bulb and rescrewed the lamp, fusing Abe's apartment and the passage lights.

He was feeling very confident. Fuentes had said the Jew was without spine, and would faint at the sight of a gun. Pedro had brought with him not only the gun Fuentes had given him, but also a flashlight.

'Stay still!' he barked, snapping on the flashlight, letting the beam take in the gun in his hand while it lit up Abe who was struggling to sit up. 'Throw the bag to me!'

Abe had been rent collecting for a long time. He had never experienced a hold-up. A cop had warned him, 'Abe, there's always a first time. Your people want you to carry a gun. Here's your permit, and here's the gun. I'll show you how to handle it.' And the cop was a good teacher. Never believing he would need the gun, Abe told himself that if a hold-up did happen and the thief got away with the rent money, he would not only lose his job, but also his home. His boss had spelt it out: 'Deliver or you're out.' So Abe took the gun talk seriously. He had never fired the gun, but he knew what to do: safety catch off, both hands on the gun and squeeze the trigger.

'Hurry!' Pedro snarled out of the darkness. 'The bag!'

By now, Abe was sitting up, clutching the bag and staring at the bright light, seeing nothing of the man shouting at him.

'Take it,' he said, and pushed the bag in the direction of the voice. The bag, heavy, travelled only a couple of feet across the coarse, worn carpet.

Pedro stared at the bag, feeling a surge of triumph run through him. Tomorrow, Anita and he would be on a plane, going home. How happy his father would be to see him again! His mind moved like quicksilver. It had been arranged that as soon as he got the money, he would dart up to the first floor where Fuentes had a one-room apartment. The Jew, scared witless, would imagine he had rushed out of the building, and when the cops were called, they would be scouring the streets for a man carrying a brown bag. Then another thought dropped into Pedro's mind. Suppose he didn't go to Fuentes' apartment, but ran into the street? Suppose he kept all the money? Forty-two hundred dollars! He would have to silence the Jew. A knock on the head! That was it! Then he would walk out, go home, and there was nothing Fuentes could do about it.

As he moved towards the bag, quivering with excitement, he took his eyes off Abe, sending the beam of his flashlight directly on the bag. Abe's hand crept inside his jacket. His fingers closed over the butt of the gun. He drew the gun as Pedro snatched up the bag.

Abe's thumb drew back the safety catch, lifted the gun and squeezed the trigger. The flash and the bang in the darkness made both men rear back. Pedro felt a seering hot something cross his cheek, then he felt his cheek turn wet. He jerked up his gun, and in panic, squeezed the trigger. The light of his flashlight centred on Abe who was struggling to his feet. Pedro felt the gun jerk in his hand, heard the bang, then with terror, saw a splodge of blood appear in the middle of Abe's forehead, saw Abe jerk and fall back.

Pedro, stunned by the noise of the two shots, stood motionless, scarcely breathing, knowing he had killed the Jew.

Into his mind, came the terrifying thought that he had killed a man! You pull a gun trigger and a man dies! Ice-cold panic seized him. He thought only of himself. If he was caught, he would spend the rest of his days behind bars: a caged animal! There would be no Anita, no welcoming father, no hot sun on the sugar cane farm.

He heard voices. Doors slammed open. A woman screamed.

Fuentes! He must get to him! Snatching up the bag in his left hand, holding the gun in his right hand, aware of blood dripping down his face, he moved out of Abe's apartment, trying to control his panic.

Fuentes, waiting at his half open door heard the two shots and he cringed. He heard doors opening. He saw a number of the first-floor tenants come crowding out onto the upper corridor.

The goddamn fool had screwed up the job! Pray the Lord, he hadn't killed the Jew! He joined the group of people who were staring down the staircase well, talking loud, a woman wailing. He saw Pedro, blood on his face, staring up at him, and he stepped back.

Pedro looked up at the frightened faces, staring down at him, and he knew this was no way of escape. Still holding the brown leather bag, he ran to the entrance of the street.

* * *

Lepski was accepting the big carton which Harry put on the bar.

'There's the chicken, Tom, plus noodles. Have a lovely meal.'

Lepski beamed.

'Man! Will this stand Carroll on her ear! Thanks a

43

million.' As Marian slid off the stool, he patted her rump. Then he heard pistol shots.

Instantly, Lepski became all-cop. He was off his stool and darting to the exit. He had his gun in his hand as he reached the street.

Already the sound of the shots had caused a commotion. Cars with screaming tyres, were pulling up. People were gaping, stopping and staring at the entrance of the highrise.

At this moment, Pedro came out onto the street. The sight of blood streaming down his face and the gun in his hand made the crowd scatter. Women began to scream, some men dived to the sidewalk.

Lepski looked across the street and saw Pedro as he began to run. Lepski, moving fast, dodging around the stopped cars, went after him.

Pedro heard the hammering sound of pursuing feet. His eyes, wide with terror, he glanced around and saw Lepski, weaving through the scattering crowd, after him. He knew instinctively that this man, chasing him, was a cop: he saw the gun in the man's hand. Half out of his mind with terror, he swivelled around and fired at Lepski. A black woman, rushing to a doorway for shelter took Pedro's bullet through her brain.

Lepski bawled: 'Stop or you're dead!'

Pedro swerved and began to dart across the street.

Holding his gun in both hands, his feet spread apart, Lepski squeezed off a shot.

Pedro felt the slam of the bullet which pitched him forward. He dropped the worn brown leather bag and the gun Fuentes had lent him slid out of his hand. He folded down, pain raging through him.

A patrol car screamed to a halt. Two cops joined Lepski. They approached Pedro cautiously, then one of the cops said, 'The sonofabitch is still alive.'

Fuentes had rushed back to his apartment, slammed the door shut and rushed to the window. Leaning out, he was in time to see Lepski shoot Pedro. He saw the brown leather bag, containing forty-two hundred dollars, drop by Pedro's fallen body, then he saw his gun lying a yard away.

The gun!

Fuentes didn't give a damn about Pedro. He only hoped he was dead, but the gun . . . !

He must have been out of his mind to have lent his gun to Pedro! As soon as the cops had checked the gun, it would be traced to him. At one time, he had acted as night watchman on a luxury yacht, and the owner had insisted he had a gun, and had fixed it with the police. Fascinated by the gun, Fuentes had wanted to keep it. When the owner of the yacht had sailed for the Bahamas, Fuentes had told him he had accidentally dropped the gun overboard. The owner had shrugged, told him to report the loss to the police and had sailed. This Fuentes hadn't done. The gun permit ran for another eight months, by then, with the money Pedro was supposed to steal, Fuentes would be back in Havana, and to hell with the cops!

But now . . . !

It would take the cops only a few hours to check out the gun, then they would come after him.

Sweating, he watched the scene below. More patrol cars arrived. An ambulance, its siren wailing, also arrived.

Panic-stricken, Fuentes turned from the window. He had to get away before the whole highrise was searched! Rushing to his closet, he threw his few clothes into a battered suitcase. Where to go? He thought of Manuel Torres, his best friend.

Fuentes often met Manuel Torres on the waterfront. Both of them had lived in the same village, near Havana, gone to the same school, and when young, had worked together on the same sugar cane farm. Fuentes was sure he could rely on Manuel for help.

Opening his door, he peered into the corridor. His neighbours' backs were turned to him: all were staring down the well of the staircase.

Moving silently, carrying the suitcase, he reached the end of the corridor to the fire door exit. He slid back the bolt, opened the door, then glanced back. No one looked in his direction, their concentration was rooted to the lobby below.

He closed the door after him, then ran down the staircase. Moving with long, quick strides, using the narrow back alleys, he headed for the waterfront.

* * *

Two hours after the murder of Abe Levi, Sergeant Hess, a short, bulky man, in charge of the Homicide Squad, came into Chief of Police Terrell's office.

'Looks like a straight grab raid, Chief,' he said. 'Two dead. Panic shooting, I guess. So far, we haven't identified the killer. He had no papers on him. We've asked around, but no one is offering information. He's a Cuban. We're still checking him out, but Cubans stick together.'

Terrell, a large man with sandy hair flecked with white, his heavy-featured face ending in a jutting, square jaw, looked what he was: an efficient, tough police chief.

'This Cuban?'

'He could survive. Tom got him in the lungs. Right now, he's in the intensive care ward. Larry is sitting by his bedside.'

'Any lead on the gun?'

'Checking it out. We should have something any time now.'

'The Press?'

Hess grimaced.

'We don't often get two killings in a day, Chief. They are having a ball.'

'That's to be expected. You've taken the killer's finger prints?'

'They're on their way to Washington now.'

Sergeant Beigler came in.

'Got a report on the gun, Chief. It belongs to a Cuban,

46

Roberto Fuentes. He has a permit. He lives in the same highrise where Levi was killed. He's not the killer. The photo on his permit doesn't match. Max and a couple of patrolmen are on their way now to pick him up.'

'This man, Fuentes, could have sold his gun to the killer,' Terrell said, 'or he could be tied to this grab.'

'That's my thinking, Chief.'

The telephone bell rang. Beigler answered it.

'Hold it,' he said, then turning to Terrell, he went on, 'Fuentes has skipped. He's taken all his clothes. No one in the highrise knows a thing . . . of course.'

'I want him,' Terrell said. 'Get it organized, Joe.'

Beigler, who loved action, nodded.

'You'll have him, Chief.'

* * *

It was after 02.00 when Anita Certes approached Manuel Torres' fishing vessel. The waterfront, apart from a few night watchmen, was deserted. The watchmen glanced at her as she walked along, keeping in the shadows. They thought she was just another of the many whores who frequented the waterfront.

She paused when she located the fishing vessel. There was a light on in the forward cabin. She felt certain, in that cabin, she would find Fuentes.

It wasn't until Anita had returned home, after cleaning the penthouse suite, that she had turned on her transistor and had heard of the shooting.

Before she had left for work in the morning, Pedro had told her when she returned in the evening, to pack.

'We leave for Havana at ten o'clock tomorrow. Be ready.'

She had put her arms around him and hugged him.

'Dear husband, I wish with all my heart this wasn't going to happen, but you can rely on me for always.'

She had returned for her afternoon break, but Pedro wasn't there. She had rested her body, but not her mind.

47

She kept thinking of the gun Pedro had shown her. She thought of his friend, Fuentes, who had given him the gun. Pedro had said there would be no risk. She was so in love with him, she forced herself to believe there would be no risk, but she remained fearful.

Back home yet again at 22.30, hoping with desperate hope to find Pedro waiting for her, the empty little room made her heart sink. Pedro had told her to pack, so wearily, she packed two suitcases to contain their few belongings. As she packed, she thought that tomorrow at this time, they would be back on the small sugar cane farm, and she would once again be slaving in the heat, but what did that matter so long as she had Pedro, her loved one, by her side?

While waiting for Pedro to return, she switched on the news. She listened to the account of the murders of Abe Levi, a rent collector and Carry Smith, a black woman, the attempt to steal the rent money which Abe Levi had collected, and her body turned to stone.

The announcer went on, 'Detective Tom Lepski, seeing the thief escaping, shouted a warning, then fired. The thief, a young Cuban, so far has not been identified. Seriously wounded, he is now in hospital, under police guard.'

Anita put her hands to her mouth, stifling a scream. Pedro!

'The police want to question a Cuban named Roberto Fuentes who is missing. The murder gun has been traced to him, and it is thought he has either sold or lent the gun to the killer.' The announcer went on. 'Anyone knowing this man's whereabouts should call police headquarters.'

Anita switched the transistor off.

Some women have steel in them: some don't. Anita had this steel which was built in her by hard, grinding work in the sugar cane fields and her work at the hotel. Once she had absorbed the shock of knowing her beloved was critically wounded, and in the hands of the police, she considered the problem. Soon the police would find out who Pedro was and where he lived. They would come to this room and question her. The Press would hound her. She would lose her job at the hotel. She must act at once!

Fuentes! He would know the police would be looking for him and he would go into hiding.

Anita had lived in Seacomb many months. She was part of the Cuban community. She knew Pedro's friends. She knew Fuentes was always talking about his rich friend, Manuel Torres who had a fishing vessel moored to the West Quai.

She had heard much about Manuel Torres. It was said he was a man of great influence. He was more than that. The Cuban community regarded him as the godfather of all the Cubans living in the city. When someone had a problem, he went to Manuel who helped him. He was known as 'The Man of Truth'. When he said he could solve a problem, it was solved. Naturally, he charged a few cents for his time, but that was accepted because his advice was always good. When he wasn't fishing, he ran a stall on the quay, selling tourist junk successfully.

While Fuentes and Pedro had drunk cheap wine, Anita, sitting with them, had listened to Fuentes boasting.

'Manuel is my friend,' he had declared to Pedro. 'If ever I got into trouble, I would go to him and he would help me.'

Manuel Torres, known as The Man of Truth! Anita thought. I will find Fuentes with him.

For more than an hour, she sat motionless, her mind busy.

Pedro must be rescued! Pedro must never serve a long term in prison! This was an unbearable, impossible thought! She well knew the value of friendship. Neither Fuentes nor Manuel would raise a finger to help Pedro unless there was a big incentive.

At the end of that desperate hour of thinking, she finally arrived at a solution. She hesitated, wondering if such a plan could succeed, then she persuaded herself there was no other way to rescue Pedro so her plan must succeed.

She would go to Manuel and Fuentes and tell them of this plan. She felt hopeful that once they grasped what enormous money they would gain, they would help to rescue her husband.

Now, she stood looking at Manuel's fishing vessel. She saw a shadow move behind the curtain of the lighted forward cabin.

She looked around, found a pebble and threw it against the lighted window.

She waited, then the cabin door opened and the shadowy figure of a giant of a man came on deck.

'It's me . . . Anita Certes,' she called softly.

Three

Mike Bannion paid off the taxi that had brought him from the Miami airport to the Seaview Hotel. He paused to look at the hotel entrance, and at the balconies ornamented by old-fashioned wrought iron. He decided this was a residential hotel for the retired with not too much money. Mentally shrugging, he walked up the few steps and into the lobby, decorated with dwarf palm trees in tarnished copper pots, and across to the modest reception desk.

A neatly dressed, elderly man gave him a smile of welcome.

'Mr. Vance is expecting me,' Mike said.

'Mr. Lucas?'

'That's me.' Mike's brother had told him to book in as Ted Lucas, and a reservation had been made for him in that name.

'A moment, please.' The elderly man used the telephone, muttered, listened, then hung up.

'Mr. Vance will see you, Mr. Lucas. First floor. Room two. Your room is on the fourth floor. Number twelve. If you will leave your bag, I'll have it taken to your room.'

Mike took the elevator to the first floor. These days, he spared himself every unnecessary effort. He found climbing stairs now gave him a sharp pain in his side. Today was a bad day. It was probably due to the flight and humping his bag. He was confident that tomorrow, he wouldn't know he had this deadly thing gnawing away inside him. The pain came and went. There were days when he tried to assure himself he wasn't going to die in a few months, but on leaving the airport, when the sharp teeth of pain bit into him, he accepted the fact that he was kidding himself.

He knocked on the door of Room 2, and a querulous voice shouted for him to come in.

Opening the door, he entered a small sitting-room, shabby, but comfortable, a room in which the very old could relax while waiting to die.

Lu Bradey sat in a wheel-chair. Looking at him, Mike saw a small, thin man who was apparently nudging eighty years of age. Bradey's disguise was yet another of his masterpieces. The shock of white hair, the big white moustache, the pinched nostrils, the dry wrinkled skin had Maggie completely fooled. Bradey had told her to come to the Seaview Hotel where there was a reservation for her in the name of Stella Jacques, and she was to ask for Mr. Vance.

When Maggie had arrived the previous afternoon and had come to Room 2, she had stared at this old man in the wheel-chair, then flustered, she had exclaimed, 'Oh, excuse me! I guess I've come to the wrong room,' and began to back out.

'Come on in, honey, and take your pants off,' Bradey said in his normal voice.

Maggie was so shocked she didn't think this was at all funny. It took Bradey quite a time to soothe her down and convince her this old cripple, patting her, was really the love of her life.

Finally, he got her down to business. He had told her the following morning the man who was to play such an important part in the hotel robbery would be arriving.

'I want you to stay in the bedroom, Maggie,' Bradey said. 'Keep the door half open and listen. I want you to make sure you can work with this man, as I am going to make sure. Haddon tells me he is okay, but he's an

52

amateur. He has no record, and I distrust amateurs. If he lets us down, loses his nerve, we are both in real trouble. Listen to his voice, and to what he says, then come in and take a long look at him. If you are nervous of him, run your fingers through your hair. If you feel sure you can work with him, then say so.'

Maggie, looking pop-eyed, nodded.

'This is a big deal, isn't it, Lu? I'm a bit worried. I wouldn't want to go to jail, but if you say it's going to be okay, then it's okay with me.'

'You won't go to jail, baby, nor will I.'

Maggie began stroking Bradey's hand.

'You know something, honey? I've never been screwed by a man of eighty. Shall we try?'

Bradey laughed.

'No. It's taken me three hours to fix this disguise. I'm not having you chewing me to bits. Go, cool off.'

Standing in the doorway, Mike regarded this old man in the wheel-chair. He was as fooled as Maggie had been and he thought: 'God! Is this decrepit old creep the man I have to work with?'

While Mike was staring, Bradey was also staring with cold, searching eyes, then he began to relax. This was quite a man, he thought. Not only tough, but he oozed discipline. Haddon had said he was an army sergeant. This wasn't a man who would lose his nerve. The sunken eyes bothered Bradey, but the firm mouth and the strong jaw line balanced out the eyes.

'I'm Mike Bannion,' the man said. 'Mr. Vance?'

'Come in and sit down,' Bradey said.

He waited until Bannion had closed the door and had sat in a chair near where Bradey's wheel-chair was positioned.

'So you're Mike Bannion,' Bradey said in his old man's voice. 'Tell me about yourself.'

Mike looked directly at Bradey. There was something phony about this old man. This, he felt instinctively.

'I'm here to do a job,' he said. 'You don't want to know

about me as I don't want to know about you. What's the job?'

Bradey liked this. This big soldier obviously meant business, he told himself, but he decided to probe further.

'I've been told you are a good shot. How good a shot are you?'

'Suppose we stop this crap?' Mike said. 'Tell whoever it is in the other room to come on out. Let's get down to business.'

Maggie came from the bedroom, paused to regard Mike, then clasped her hands.

'What a gorgeous hunk of man!' she exclaimed.

Bradey laughed, seeing Mike was staring at Maggie.

'Let's all have a drink,' he said, and getting from his wheelchair, he walked to the bottles lined up on the table. 'This is Maggie. She's working with us. What'll you have, Mike?'

Stunned by the sudden activity of an old cripple and the sight of Maggie, looking her sexiest, Mike just gaped. Then pulling himself together, he got to his feet.

'Scotch?' Bradey asked.

'What the hell is all this?' Mike demanded.

'Have a Scotch, Mike,' Bradey said, pouring a big shot. 'Maggie, you had better lay off. I know Scotch ruins your concentration. Give Mike his drink while I make mine.'

Maggie took the glass and crossed to Mike.

'Here you are, big man,' she said.

He took the glass, thinking he had never seen such a sexy-looking woman. His mind was in a slight daze, then seeing Bradey was waving him to a chair, he sat down.

'Okay, Mike, sorry to have conned you, but I wanted to be sure you were the right man for the job,' Bradey said as he sat in his wheel-chair. 'I'm satisfied.' He looked at Maggie. 'How about you?'

Maggie sighed.

'Oh yes. He's all gorgeous muscle!'

Bradey laughed.

'You'll have to get used to Maggie. It took me time to get used to her myself.'

By now, Mike had recovered from the shock of seeing this aged man behave like a thirty-year-old and to Maggie's impact.

'Mr. Vance,' he said in his curt military voice, 'I asked what this job is.'

Maggie moaned softly.

'Isn't that a wonderful voice?' she said, fluttering her eyelashes.

'Maggie, will you shut up?' Bradey snapped, then turning to Mike, he went on, 'Here's what we are going to do. I'm acting as a cripple, Maggie is my nurse, you are my chauffeur.' He paused, then asked, 'You've got the uniform?'

'I've got it.'

'Fine. Here's the dope.'

For the next twenty minutes, Bradey explained the details of the steal.

'Your job is to put the guards out of action if they show up. You will use a dart gun,' Bradey concluded and signalled to Maggie who went into the bedroom and returned with the gun. 'There must be no mistake,' Bradey went on as Mike examined the gun. 'It isn't lethal. No one dies. The trick is to get the dart into the necks of the guards. That's your job, then you help me to unload the boxes from the safe and for this you get paid fifty thousand dollars.'

Mike nodded.

'Right. You asked me if I was a good shot,' he said. 'That's a fair enough question when it involves fifty thousand dollars.' He looked around the room. 'That picture on the wall.' He pointed to a copy of an impressionist in faded colours. It hung some twenty feet from where he was sitting. 'The boy on the left: his right eye . . . get it?'

Both Bradey and Maggie turned to stare at the painting. For the first time, they were aware that it was on the wall.

Mike lifted the gun. His movement was swift and confident. There was a plopping sound as he squeezed the trigger.

'Take a look,' he said.

Bradey left his wheel-chair, crossed the room and peered at the painting. In the right eye of the boy was the drugged dart.

* * *

The time was 11.40. The waiters of the Spanish Bay Hotel were circulating around the big swimming-pool with trays of various cocktails, responding to the flicking fingers of the rich who lay in the sun chairs. The waiters were followed by well-trained boys carrying trays of delicious *canapés*.

Wilbur Warrenton had had his morning's swim. By his side, his wife, Maria, in a bikini, was reading a novel. Swimming in the morning was not for her. Her make-up and hair style were so elaborate, she swam only in the evening when she could spend an hour or more restoring the ravages of water before a late dinner.

Wilbur had finished his second dry martini. He was feeling relaxed. So far, his honeymoon had been a success. The hotel was everything it claimed to be. The service was impeccable and the cuisine was as good as any of the three-star Paris restaurants. The one small cloud on the otherwise sunny horizon was Maria's increasing complaints. Utterly spoilt, she was the kind of woman who always found some fault whatever luxury was provided. Her present complaint was there were too many old people residing at the hotel.

Wilbur pointed out that the Spanish Bay was the most expensive and best hotel in the world. Only the old could afford to stay there.

'We're lucky my father is paying for us, Maria,' he said, 'otherwise we wouldn't be here.'

Maria had sniffed.

'It's like living in a graveyard.'

'We can always move. Would you like that? We could go to the Rivage where there are young people.'

'The Rivage? Are you crazy? It's a slum!'

Wilbur, glancing at his watch, stood up.

'I'm just going to call Dad.'

Maria frowned.

'Oh, God! Not again? Do you have to telephone him every day?'

'He likes a chat,' Wilbur said. 'I won't be long.'

He strode away while Maria shrugged and returned to her novel.

Wilbur also liked a brief talk with his father, and he knew the old man looked forward to telling his son the daily business happenings. Wilbur knew his father was lonely, and was longing for him to return to Dallas and to provide him with grandchildren. Uneasily, Wilbur had told Maria that his father had bought a *de luxe* house for them, fully furnished, with staff, two cars, swimming-pool and a small park. In fact, everything money could buy.

'Who wants to live in a hole like Dallas?' she had demanded crossly. 'After our honeymoon, I want to go to Paris and Venice.'

'I'll be working in Dallas, Maria,' Wilbur said, patiently. 'You'll like it. I've seen the house. It's really wonderful! We'll go to Paris later.'

She had given him her stubborn stare and had said nothing. Taking the elevator to his penthouse suite, Wilbur entered the living-room and put a call through to Dallas. In a few minutes, he was talking to his father.

'Hi, son!' Silas Warrenton's bass voice boomed over the line. 'How's it going?'

'Fine, Dad, and you?'

'Plenty of business. Dow Jones is up for a change. I've just sold a parcel of stock: got me a nice profit. I'm lunching with a couple of Arabs: big shots in their neck of the woods, but peanuts to me. They are trying to promote a deal. If I get it on my terms, could be worth real money.'

'Good for you, Dad.'

'Well, this old codger keeps the pot boiling.' A pause, then, 'How's your wife?' Silas seldom called Maria by her name.

'Fine, Dad.'

'Got her pregnant yet?'

Wilbur forced a laugh.

'Give us time, Dad. Maria wants to see a bit of the world before embarking on a family.'

He heard his father give a grunt of disapproval.

'Don't leave it too long, son. I'm not getting any younger. When are you coming home?'

'Oh, about a couple of weeks.'

'I've got all kinds of interesting things lined up for you. I want you to take some of the work-load off my back, son. Did you tell your wife about the house? I took a look at it. It's pretty fancy.'

'Sure, Dad, I told her.' Wilbur struggled to put enthusiasm into his voice. 'She's pleased.'

Again the grunt.

'So she should be. It cost three million.' A pause, then, 'Well, enjoy yourself, son. I've got a board in a moment, and you'll be on that board with me pretty soon. So long, son, take care,' and Silas hung up.

Anita Certes had been finishing Maria's bathroom when Wilbur had walked in and began talking to his father. Hurriedly, she had pushed the door to and listened. The one-sided telephone conversation didn't give her any information except that the easy warmth of Wilbur's voice told her that what she had heard from the staff gossip that Silas Warrenton, enormously rich, and his son were fond of each other. One of the Cuban waiters who serviced the penthouse had told her from what he had overheard, the old man longed for grandchildren. 'That rich bitch won't play. I heard them arguing in the bedroom. She's too selfish to have children. The son will take over the oil kingdom. He'll be worth billions when the old man croaks,' the waiter had told her.

Anita had had no sleep. She had spent hours in the stuffy forward cabin of Manuel Torres' fishing vessel, talking.

First, she had begged Fuentes to help Pedro. He had shrugged.

'What can I do? The cops are looking for me!' he had said, his voice shrill. 'If I could raise some money, I'll go back to Havana, but I'm stuck.'

'You will be safe here,' Manuel said. 'I don't desert my friends.'

'Isn't my husband your friend?' Anita demanded.

'His friend,' Manuel said, nodding at Fuentes. 'Not mine.'

Fuentes waved his hands in despair.

'I can't do a thing! Don't you understand? The cops have got him! He's wounded. What can I do?'

Leaning forward, her eyes burning, Anita told him.

The two men listened while she talked, then suddenly, Fuentes interrupted.

'This is crazy talk!' he exploded. 'You're out of your head! Go away! Don't come here again! You're mad!'

Manuel laid a restraining hand on Fuentes' arm.

'I can see possibilities,' he said. 'Let us examine this idea. Calm yourself.'

'It's crazy talk!'

'Nothing involving five million dollars is crazy talk to me. Calm yourself.'

Anita watched the two men. She had expected opposition. Fuentes was stupid, but she could tell that Manuel was nibbling at the bait she was dangling. She regarded him: big, powerful, with a bushy black beard, a completely bald head and small, cruel eyes. If she could only convince him, she felt confident he would handle her plan well.

Manuel looked at her.

'Let me understand this,' he said. 'Your idea is for us to take over the penthouse suite at the hotel and hold Warrenton and his wife to ransom?'

'That is my plan,' Anita said quietly. 'Warrenton is worth billions. His father loves him. A five-million ransom would mean nothing to him.'

'And how do we take over the penthouse?' Manuel asked.

'I tell you she's crazy!' Fuentes shouted angrily. 'I know the hotel. There, they have security guards! Take over the penthouse . . . crazy talk!'

Manuel patted Fuentes' arm.

'My friend, I ask you to keep quiet. Let us listen. Five million dollars! Think what that would mean.' Looking at Anita, he again asked, 'And how do we take over the penthouse?'

'Through me,' Anita said. 'I work at the hotel. There's nothing I don't know about the security, how to reach the penthouse, how to avoid the guards and the house detective.' She turned to Fuentes. 'The cops are looking for you. Are you going to stay in this cabin for months? Can't you realize once in the penthouse you can ask for anything: food, drink, cigarettes . . . anything, and because you hold the Warrentons, the hotel will give you what you ask for. Then when the ransom is handed over, we all, taking the Warrentons as hostages, leave for home with five million dollars.'

Fuentes gaped at her, then looked uneasily at Manuel.

'Yes. Maybe,' he said slowly. 'You are sure you can get us into the penthouse?'

Anita began to relax. Another fish was nibbling at her bait.

'I can,' she said. 'I have duplicates of the keys to the staff door and the penthouse.'

'You have?' Manuel said sharply. 'How did you get them?'

Sometime in the past, Pedro had told her, 'Always have

duplicates of hotel keys. You never know when you might need them.' And he had told her how to make a wax impression and he had arranged to get the keys cut.

'That is my business,' she said. 'I have them.'

Fuentes looked at Manuel.

'What do you think?'

'I like it. We will need a third man. We don't know how long we will be penned up in that place. We have to sleep. One on, one off is dangerous. We will need a third man.'

'I will be the third man,' Anita said.

Manuel shook his head.

'No. It is better for you to keep out of this.'

'I will be the third man,' Anita said firmly. 'Before long, the cops will find out the name of my husband. They will come after me, and I will lose my job. When that happens, there will be no way for you to reach the penthouse. This has to be done quickly.'

Manuel thought about this, then nodded.

'She makes sense,' he said to Fuentes. 'Let me think carefully about this plan of yours, Mrs. Certes. Tomorrow night, come here and I will tell you if we will do this.'

'Not later than tomorrow night.'

'Tomorrow night. It will be either yes or no,' Manuel said. She had them hooked, she thought, then looking directly at Manuel, she said, 'Now listen. I will get you into the penthouse on one condition.'

Both men looked suspiciously at her.

'And what is the condition?' Manuel asked.

'I don't want any of the ransom money. Whatever you get is for you two to divide, but the ransom demand must include the release and safe conduct of Pedro to come with us when we take the hostages to Havana. If you don't agree to this condition, I will not get you into the penthouse.'

Fuentes again exploded.

'I told you she was crazy!' he screamed at Manuel.

'Pedro is wounded! He could be dying! The cops will never release him! He has killed twice! This is mad talk!'

'Shut up!' Manuel barked, losing patience. 'Now Mrs. Certes, this is a very difficult condition, but not impossible. Once we get into the penthouse and are in control, then we will be able to dictate terms. I promise you I will do my best to have your husband with us when we leave. I am a man of my word. I am known as a man of truth. I give you my promise, but it will be difficult.'

'Manuel Torres,' Anita said, her eyes hard and cold. 'I am not a stupid woman. My only thought is to have back the light of my life . . . Pedro. When the time comes, and if I am not satisfied that they will release Pedro, then I will kill that rich South American bitch and will kill Warrenton too unless they do agree to release Pedro. This is what you will tell them, and if they don't believe you, then I will also tell them and they will believe me!'

Manuel regarded her, startled. Here, he thought, was a woman of great strength, and he felt a surge of admiration run through him. He was completely convinced she meant what she was saying.

He stood for a long moment, looking at her, then he nodded. The steel in Anita's voice convinced him.

'Yes, it could work. Come tomorrow night. I have many contacts. I will make inquiries. First, we must find out about your husband's condition. That will be no problem. Tomorrow night, when you have finished work, we will discuss what we have to do.'

Wearily, but triumphant, Anita got to her feet, and Manuel, rising to his great height, held out his hand.

'You are a good wife and a fine woman,' he said. 'We will work well together.'

When she had gone, Fuentes burst out, 'She's crazy!'

Manuel regarded him, then shook his head.

'She is in love. When women are truly in love, they are stronger than men. Now, we sleep.'

* * *

Claude Previn was the day duty reception clerk at the Spanish Bay Hotel. His work entailed welcoming arrivals, signing them in, arranging for them to be conducted to their suites or chalets and preparing accounts. Aged thirty-five, tall, lean and darkly handsome, Previn had worked for some years at the George V Hotel, Paris, as a minor reception clerk. Advised by his father who ran a two-star restaurant on the Left Bank, he had applied for the position of first reception clerk. Accepted, Previn had been working in this best of all hotels for the past two years. Jean Dulac, the owner of the hotel, was pleased with him. Previn's future appeared to be assured.

On this hot sunny morning, Previn was at the reception desk, surveying the vast lounge where a number of elderly people sat, talking and having their late morning cocktails. He listened to the nasal chatter of these rich old people and he thought longingly of the George V Hotel where the action was. Here, there were mostly old people who were demanding, but content to eat, drink and gossip. The old rich, Previn thought, were utterly dull, but without them, this great hotel wouldn't exist.

A vision in white appeared before him. For a moment, he blinked, not believing that he was looking at the most gorgeous, sexy woman he had ever seen.

Maggie Schultz, attired in a nurse's uniform, her honey-coloured hair, except for stray curls, concealed by a nurse's head-dress, her big, sexy eyes glittering, was to Previn, even clothed, better than any *Playboy* fold-in.

Maggie, with her sexual awareness, regarded this handsome man, knowing she had made a big impact.

'Mr. Cornelius Vance has a reservation,' she said in her demure voice.

For a long moment, Previn could only stare at her, then, pulling himself together, he bowed, thinking if there was one woman in the world he wanted to bed with, it was this woman, standing, smiling at him.

'Mr. Vance. Of course. Chalet three,' he said, his voice husky.

'Well, he's right outside,' Maggie said. 'The poor dear can't come in. He told me to sign him in. I'm his nurse: Stella Jacques.' She released her sexiest smile. 'What do I do?'

Previn, almost hypnotized by the smile, flicked his fingers. Two bell boys appeared as if by magic.

'If you would please sign in for Mr. Vance, Miss Jacques,' he said. 'These two will conduct you to the chalet.'

Maggie signed the register, then gave Previn another sexy smile and followed the bell boys to where the Rolls waited.

Previn drew in a deep breath. What a woman! he thought. As he was watching her cross the lobby, marvelling at the swing of her neat buttocks, a voice, speaking in French, said, 'Who is she, Claude?'

Previn started guiltily and turned.

'Good morning, Mr. Dulac,' he said, and respectfully bowed his head.

Jean Dulac, owner of this *de luxe* hotel, was on the sunny side of fifty years of age, tall, distinguished-looking with that polished charm that is unique with the French, but behind this charm lurked a ruthless efficiency that had brought about the miracle of the Spanish Bay Hotel. He tolerated no slackness, nor lazy service. He had created his hotel as the best in the world, and he was determined that the hotel would remain the best. He left the running of the hotel to highly paid experts, but he supervised, correcting and suggesting.

Each morning, at 09.30, he left his office and visited every department of the hotel, smiling, apparently kindly, but constantly checking for possible faults. He began with the laundry, having a nice word with the women who adored him, then he went to the wine cellars, talking with the wine master who had come from France, then he visited the three restaurants, discussed the day's

menus with the *maître d's*, then to the kitchen to talk to
the chief chef, a quick look around, smiling at the young
chefs, but always checking.

The morning's ritual took time. Finally, he came into
the lounge and spoke, with his Maurice Chevalier accent,
to the rich oldies who were charmed.

Moving to the reception desk, he asked again, 'Who
was she?'

'Mr. Cornelius Vance has just arrived, sir,' Previn said.
'That was his nurse.'

'Ah, yes. Mr. Vance: a cripple.' Dulac smiled. 'He
knows how to choose a nurse, apparently.'

Previn inclined his head.

'So it seems, sir.'

Dulac nodded, then walked out onto the terrace to
pause, say a word, then move on to his other rich clients
around the swimming-pool.

Installed in a *de luxe* chalet, not without a slight
commotion of getting the crippled Mr. Vance out of the
Rolls, and into his wheel-chair, Bradey, Maggie and Mike
looked around and grinned at each other.

The bell boys had gone. The offer to unpack had been
dismissed by Maggie. There were two bottles of champagne in ice buckets, flowers and a big basket of assorted
fruits on the sideboard to welcome them.

'Very fancy,' Bradey said. 'This is something I dig:
luxury at someone else's expense. Mike, bust open one of
those bottles. We may as well take advantage of this joint
while we can.'

Maggie had dashed around, exploring the chalet finding
three bedrooms, three bathrooms and a tiny kitchenette.

As Mike was wrestling with the champagne cork, she
came back into the living-room.

'It's quite, quite groovy!' she exclaimed. 'Come and
look!'

'This is the best hotel in the world,' Bradey said. 'Let's
have a drink.'

While they sipped the champagne, Bradey said, 'Maggie, we mustn't waste time. I want you to circulate. You know what your job is. We must find out where the safe is located.'

'I've already made a contact,' Maggie said. 'The reception clerk is gorgeous. If I can get him alone for ten minutes, he's a dead duck.'

'Then fix it, baby, to get him alone.'

* * *

Anita walked up the gang-plank of Manuel's fishing vessel. She saw Manuel, outlined against the light of the forward cabin. He had been waiting for her, and he raised his hand in greeting.

In the stuffy cabin, with Fuentes nervously nibbling at his nails, Anita sank wearily onto the bench, resting her hands on the greasy table on which Manuel took his meals.

'I have been organizing this affair,' Manuel said, sitting opposite her. 'First, I have news of your husband. He is still unconscious, but he will live. He has every attention. You don't have to worry about him.'

Anita clenched her hands and closed her eyes. Watching her, Manuel saw her dedicated love for this stupid, worthless man, and he marvelled at it.

'The cops are trying to find out who he is,' Manuel went on, 'but they have come up against a wall of silence. I have told our people not to talk to the cops. Even when Pedro recovers consciousness, he won't talk. So the situation is encouraging. We now have time to get your plan moving. This is a good thing, because nothing should be rushed.'

Anita looked searchingly at him.

'Will my husband live?'

'Yes. One of the hospital interns is a good friend of mine. He says Pedro is badly ill, but he will live.'

Tears trickled down Anita's face which she impatiently brushed away.

'And so . . . ?'

'We must wait a little while until Pedro is well enough to travel. It would be a stupid act to be too hasty. If we move him from the intensive care ward too soon, he might not survive,' Manuel said quietly. 'You see? I think not only of the money, but of your husband.'

Anita nodded.

'Very well,' Manuel continued. 'I have been giving this affair much thought. We must put on pressure. This pressure must be so strong, the cops will be forced to hand over Pedro.'

'Pressure?' Anita looked puzzled. 'What pressure? I don't understand.'

'Warrenton's father will pay the ransom. Five million dollars will mean nothing to him, but to get Pedro released is a much bigger problem,' Manuel said. 'I have thought about it. The cops will resist, so great pressure must be brought to bear.'

'What pressure? I still don't understand.'

'The Spanish Bay Hotel is the best and the finest hotel in the world. To the tourists, it is a status symbol. Even when they don't stay at the hotel, I understand from my informants, they are asked if they have dined at the hotel. They suffer a loss of face if they have to admit they haven't: such is the snobbery of the rich. I have talked to one of the workers, a good friend of mine, who works at the City Hall. He tells me the city's revenue would be nearly halved if the Spanish Bay Hotel didn't exist. The owner of the hotel, Dulac, is a personal friend of the mayor. Now when Dulac learns there is a powerful bomb hidden somewhere in the hotel, and unless he can persuade the mayor and the police to release Pedro, the bomb will explode, he will do his utmost to get Pedro released. He will be told that this bomb could and will create such damage, his hotel will be out of action for months.'

'But suppose the mayor and the police don't react to your bluff?' Anita said.

Manuel smiled evilly.

'I never bluff. This will be for real, and you will have to find a safe place to conceal the bomb.'

Anita's eyes opened wide.

'You have a bomb?'

Manuel nodded.

'I will have two bombs in a few days. I have many grateful friends. I have talked to a man who, but for me, would be serving a thirty-year jail sentence. He is an explosive expert. I have explained what I want. At this moment, he is constructing the bombs: one is a very minor affair. It will cause little damage: break a few windows, nothing important, but the second bomb will create havoc. Once we are in the penthouse, all I have to do is to press one of two buttons and the little bomb will go off by radio beam. This will tell Dulac, I am not bluffing. If I press the second button, the hotel will cease to function for many months.'

Anita flushed with excitement.

'This is a wonderful plan! You are truly a man of truth! Where do I hide these bombs?'

'That is a good question. The little bomb should be hidden in the entrance hall of the hotel. It is not powerful enough to injure anyone, but it will be noisy, and glass will break.'

'The big bomb?'

'This is something I have given a lot of thought about. I have asked myself where is the heart of the hotel that keeps a hotel running? The kitchens! If we threaten to wipe out the kitchens, Dulac will realize his beautiful hotel will come to a standstill, so you will conceal the big bomb somewhere very, very safe, in the kitchens.'

Anita drew in a deep breath.

'That will not be easy. There is a day staff and a night staff, always on duty. The kitchens never close.'

'If you want your husband you must solve this problem. There is time. Think about it. I can think of no other way to get Pedro's release. It is the only way.'

Anita sat motionless, thinking, then she nodded. She got to her feet.

'I will find such a hiding place,' she said. 'You are a clever man.' She put her hand on Manuel's shoulder. 'Thank you.'

When she had gone, Fuentes exclaimed, 'Who cares about this jerk, Pedro? Five million dollars! To hell with this bomb idea. It's crazy!'

'If it is possible, Pedro leaves with us,' Manuel said coldly, 'I have given her my word. That is final.'

'Now, wait,' Fuentes said. 'Think about this. Who wants to have anything to do with bombs? Don't you see . . .'

Manuel interrupted him.

'Then go, my friend. Go out onto the harbour and get picked up by the cops. You either work with me, do what I say or you are at liberty to go.'

Fuentes sat still for a long moment. He realized he had no alternative but to accept Manuel's conditions.

'Then I work with you,' he said finally.

Manuel leaned forward and slapped Fuentes on his shoulder.

'Well said. We drink to it.' His cold little eyes stared fixedly at Fuentes, 'And remember, my friend, when I drink with a man who tells me he will work with me, it is a binding contract. Is that understood?'

The two men stared at each other, then Fuentes forced a smile.

'It is understood,' he said.

* * *

With the aid of six detectives borrowed from the Miami police force, the eight detectives of Paradise City were combing Seacomb, searching for Fuentes. They also carried a photograph of Pedro, taken as he lay unconscious in the hospital bed. No one knew him. No one had ever seen him: nor had they seen Fuentes, nor knew him. Manuel Torres' word had gone out.

The Cuban workers followed Manuel's instructions. One day, he told them, they too could be in cop trouble. The wall of silence was frustrating to the hot, tired detectives visiting each walk-up, knocking on doors, showing photographs and asking: 'Have you seen these men?'

Lepski, with Detective 2nd Grade Max Jacoby, was working the waterfront. The hot lead to Fuentes' whereabouts was that his gun permit had been vouched for by Lu Salinsbury, a rich yacht owner who had asked for a permit so Fuentes could guard Salinsbury's big, opulent yacht. Salinsbury had left for the Bahamas, but records showed Fuentes hadn't turned in the gun. Lepski decided some of the night watchmen, guarding the other yachts, might know where Fuentes could be found.

As the two detectives walked along the waterfront, Lepski chewed on a dry cheeseburger and was grumbling. The time was 22.30, and he kept thinking of the chicken dinner he had left on Harry Atkins' bar the previous evening, when the shooting began.

'Chicken in white wine sauce and mushrooms!' he moaned as he chewed. 'Imagine!'

'Harry will keep it in the freezer for you,' Jacoby said comfortingly. 'If there's enough for three invite me to dinner.'

Lepski snorted.

'You think too much about food, Max.'

'It's not a bad occupation. How about those two?'

The two detectives slowed their pace. Two men sat on a bench, drinking beer from cans. They both wore revolvers on their hips and were obviously hired guards, guarding two big yachts moored side by side.

Lepski introduced himself, flashing his shield.

One of them, elderly and bulky, squinted at the photograph of Fuentes, then handed it to his younger companion.

'Sure, that's Fuentes,' the younger one said. 'He used to work for Mr. Salinsbury. That's right, isn't it, Jack?'

'Yeah. A Cuban.' The bulky man looked up at Lepski. 'Is he in trouble?'

'He could give us information,' Lepski said. 'Any idea where we can find him?'

'He doesn't work around here any more. Haven't seen him in weeks.'

The younger man said, 'You talk to Manuel Torres. He and Fuentes are buddies. Torres owns a fishing vessel at the far end of the harbour. Berth three. If anyone knows where Fuentes is, he will.'

'Manuel Torres?' Lepski asked. 'Who's he?'

'Just another goddamn Cuban. I've no time for Cubans, but Torres seems important. He owns his vessel and runs a junk stall in the market.'

'Important?' Lepski probed.

'To Cubans. He has lots of friends who visit his vessel.' The younger man shrugged. 'For a Cuban, I guess he's important.'

Lepski thanked the two guards, then moved along the waterfront with Jacoby at his side.

'We'll take a look at Torres,' Lepski said.

It was a long trudge, past the moored luxury yachts to the basin where the fishing vessels were moored. Both men were sweating in the humid night air, and Lepski was in an ugly mood.

A squat, dark Cuban woman walked by them, giving them a quick, suspicious glance, then looking away.

Neither of the two detectives were to know she was the wife of Pedro Certes. They dismissed her as yet another of the waterfront whores.

They found Manuel's vessel moored in the third berth, between two clam fishing boats. The gang-plank had been run in, but there was a light on in the forward cabin.

In his cop voice, Lepski bawled, 'Hi, Torres! Police!'

Manuel and Fuentes were just touching glasses of

71

whisky to cement their contract when Lepski's voice made both men slop their drinks.

Fuentes turned a greenish yellow and his eyes went dim with fear.

Police!

Manuel patted his arm.

'I will handle it.' Moving swiftly, he pushed aside the table and lifted a trap door. 'Down there, and keep silent. It will be okay. Leave it to me.'

As Fuentes lowered himself into a dark hole that stank of stale fish, Manuel came out on deck.

'You Torres?' Lepski barked.

'That is my name,' Manuel said quietly. 'What is it?'

'We want to talk to you.'

Manuel ran out the gang-plank, then moving swiftly, he arrived on the quay and faced Lepski who flashed his shield.

'Where is Roberto Fuentes?' he demanded.

'You mean my friend, Roberto Fuentes?' Manuel asked and smiled.

'You heard! We want him as accessory for murder. Know where he is?'

'Accessory for murder?' Manuel faked a startled expression, 'Ah! That explains everything. I guessed something was wrong.'

'Explains what?'

'My friend came to me last night. He seemed agitated. He told me he had to leave for Havana immediately. He asked me to lend him money. I look after my friends so I lent him a hundred dollars. When my friends are in trouble, I don't ask questions. You, Mr. Cop, when your friends are in trouble, would act the same way.' Manuel was now enjoying himself as he watched Lepski's frustrated expression. 'So my good friend, Roberto Fuentes, took a boat and is now with his family in Havana.'

'What boat?' Lepski snarled.

'That I wouldn't know. He has friends on the waterfront. Many of them fish. Some go to Havana on business.

We Cubans help each other.' Manuel shrugged. 'Boat? I wouldn't know about that.'

Lepski moved forward and tapped Manuel on his chest.

'I think Fuentes is on your scrap heap. I think you are lying.'

'Mr. Cop, I am known on the waterfront as a man of truth. You can search my poor home with pleasure,' Manuel said. 'Fuentes, I assure you, is now with his parents in Havana. You will, of course, have a search warrant? I believe that is the necessary form.'

Lepski loosened his tie.

'Now listen, smart ass, you could get caught with an accessory to murder-after-rap. That could put you away for a five-ten. I'm asking you: is Fuentes on your vessel?'

Manuel shook his head.

'He is, by now, in Havana. I am a man of truth. Ask any Cuban. Never mind the search-warrant. Come aboard. Search: satisfy yourself. I am a man of truth.'

Lepski hesitated. If he went on board and didn't find Fuentes, this slick bastard could complain to the mayor: an infringement of rights. Lepski decided he wasn't going to get involved in a mess like that. He decided he would report to his chief first.

Watching him, Manuel saw his bluff had worked.

'I need my sleep, Mr. Cop,' he said. 'I am a hard-working man. You too need your sleep. I say goodnight.'

He stepped back, gave Lepski a respectful wave of his hand, walked up the gang-plank, waved again, pulled in the gang-plank, then walked to the lighted cabin.

'He could be telling the truth,' Jacoby said.

'Like I'm Greta Garbo,' Lepski snarled.

Four

Maria Warrenton was in the mood to show off. To Wilbur's surprise, she told him they would dine in the Empress Restaurant which was strictly for the clients staying at the hotel, away from music, rich tourists, and with a terrace on its own.

'But that will be full of old people,' Wilbur said as he struggled with his tie. 'Wouldn't you like something more gay where we can dance?'

'We will dine there,' Maria said firmly. 'I want to show those stupid-looking old women I have finer and more beautiful jewels than they have.'

'As you like,' Wilbur said. 'I'll get the diamonds then.' Going to the concealed safe that Dulac had installed, he opened it and took out the red leather case. Then putting the case on the dressing-table, he finally fixed his tie. He put on his white tuxedo, then sat down to watch Maria adorn herself with the jewellery her father had given her. He admitted, watching her, she was a very beautiful woman, and the glitter of diamonds became her dark skin.

When Maggie wheeled Bradey into the Empress Restaurant, their appearance caused a minor sensation. The old people were already seated at their tables. Waiters were moving around with trays of apéritifs. The short, fat *maître d'* was darting from table to table, smiling, suggesting this and that delicacy to tempt the jaded palates of the

75

old. Seeing Maggie pushing the wheel-chair, he flicked his fingers and his assistant took the bundle of menus from him, and he advanced, smiling at Bradey.

'Mr. Vance,' he said, 'A pleasure. Your table, as requested, is in the far corner.' He flicked his fingers and a waiter approached. 'Please, Madame, allow us . . .'

'I prefer to manage,' Maggie said, giving him her sexy smile. 'Just show me the way.'

Watched by all the diners, she wheeled Bradey to a distant, secluded table.

There were muted whispers: 'Who's he?' 'Pretty nurse.' 'Must have just arrived.'

Finally, settled at the table, the *maître d'* handed Bradey and Maggie a menu each.

'If I may suggest . . .' he began.

'Go away!' Bradey growled in his old man's voice. 'I know what I like! I'm not an idiot!'

The *maître d's* smile slipped a little, but Maggie gave him a knowing wink to tell him her patient was difficult. He bowed and went away.

'Lu, pet, you don't have to be rude to the nice man,' Maggie whispered.

'Quiet, baby!' Bradey said. 'I'm in character.' Then he began to examine the menu. The prices against each dish made his eyes widen. 'What a racket!' he muttered. 'Daylight robbery!' He began to search for the cheapest dish, and finally decided on *Sole de L'Impératrice* which cost $35. 'We'll have the sole,' he told Maggie who was drooling over the Epicurean dishes.

Maggie's face fell.

'I don't dig fish, honey. I'd adore this Chicken Maryland.'

'Look at the price!'

'You told me we were going to make a million,' Maggie said. 'I'm starving!'

'If we're unlucky, I'll have to pay for your food out of my own pocket. We'll have the sole.'

76

'Unlucky?' Maggie immediately looked worried. 'You said . . .'

'Quiet!' Bradey snapped. 'Act like a nurse! You talk when I speak to you.'

Maggie sighed and began to butter a roll of bread. It wasn't until the sole arrived and was presented with a flourish that Maggie, peering at the contents of the silver dish, brightened. The sole, done in a heavy cream and wine sauce was decorated with sliced truffles, diced lobster and fried oysters.

Bradey had sternly refused the *maître d's* suggestion that they should begin with a prawn salad, and when the wine waiter offered a white wine, the price of which made Bradey cringe, he demanded water.

'If you go on stuffing yourself with bread,' Bradey said when the wine waiter had gone, 'you'll get fat.'

'I'm hungry,' Maggie whined, 'but this looks okay,' and she began to attack the sole.

As Bradey ate, he surveyed the people at the other tables.

'Ed was right,' he muttered. 'The jewels these old cows are wearing are worth a pile of dough. Look at that old trout on your right. That bracelet is worth at least a hundred thousand.'

'I didn't think I liked fish,' Maggie said, intent on her plate, 'but this is gorgeous.'

There was a sudden commotion at the entrance to the restaurant. The *maître d'* hurried forward. Two of his satellites followed.

Wilbur and Maria made their entrance.

Maria looked magnificent. Tall, her expression haughty and condescending, she wore an exclusive Balmain creation. Her glittering diamonds put all the other diamonds in the restaurant to shame.

'God almighty!' Bradey muttered. 'Look at this! What a woman! Look at that diamond collar! That's worth at least two million! Those bracelets! Three million! Her ear-rings! She must be wearing six million dollars worth of diamonds!'

Maggie was busy mopping up the fish sauce with a piece of bread. She looked up, regarded Maria as she walked to a table, then she stuffed the bread into her mouth.

'I bet she's a bitch,' she mumbled, her mouth full, 'but I'd give my eyes to have a dress like that,' and she reached for another roll.

Bradey wasn't listening. He was doing mental arithmetic. Broken up, those diamonds would fetch at least five million. He had to find out who this woman was.

At this moment, the assistant *maître d'* approached.

'I trust you enjoyed your sole, sir,' he said.

'Very nice.'

'Perhaps some cheese or dessert?'

'Dessert,' Maggie said firmly.

'Certainly, Madame.' Fingers were flicked and four, three tier trolleys, ladened with the most exotic and delicious-looking trifles, tarts, cakes and compotes arrived.

Bradey was still eyeing Maria's diamonds, his thoughts were far away. He only came back to earth when the assistant *maître d'* asked, 'And what would you care for, sir?'

Bradey stiffened and stared at Maggie's plate that was heaped with a selection of dessert that made him blink. Maggie had said softly to the serving waiter, 'Something of everything.' She prayed Bradey was too occupied to hear, and something of everything was served.

'Just coffee,' Bradey said. 'Tell me, who are those two who have just come in?'

The assistant *maître d'* beamed.

'Mr. and Mrs. Wilbur Warrenton, sir.'

'I thought I recognized them,' Bradey lied. 'Are they staying?'

The assistant *maître d'* beamed again.

'They are on their honeymoon. Yes, indeed, they will be with us for the next ten days.'

'Fine-looking couple,' Bradey said.

A waiter brought the coffee, and the assistant *maître d'*, with a bow, went to another table.

'Do you have to make such a hog of yourself?' Bradey demanded, glaring at Maggie. 'That'll cost me at least fifteen dollars!'

'Worth it,' Maggie said, rolling her eyes. She offered him a portion of rum trifle on her fork. 'Have a bit, honey. It's out of this world!'

'Eat, and shut up!' Bradey snapped.

As he stirred his coffee, he dug into his encyclopaedic memory of names. He had long ago made it his business to know the names of the super-rich who owned works of art, and it didn't take him more than a few moments to place Wilbur Warrenton. This handsome man was the son of Silas Warrenton, the Texas oil king, worth billions. No wonder this haughty-looking bitch was wearing a fortune in diamonds.

Bradey rubbed his chin, his mind very active. If he could get his hands on those diamonds, it might even be better than trying to open the hotel's safe. Although Haddon's plan had, at the time, seemed acceptable, Bradey was now not so sure. It depended on where the safe was. It could be inaccessible.

Again, he studied those flashing diamonds across the room, and he felt a lusting urge to have them. He must talk to Haddon, but first, he must find out in which suite the Warrentons were staying. Then to find out if she used the hotel's safe. So many arrogant women wouldn't be bothered to put their jewels each night in a hotel's safe, believing they were just as safe in their suites or bedrooms. Maybe Maria Warrenton was one of those.

He was still thinking, when Maggie laid down her fork with a sigh of content.

Bradey scowled at her.

'Maybe you'd like some more, Maggie?' he said sarcastically. 'Some more of the trifle?'

Maggie's eyes opened wide.

'It really is gorgeous. Perhaps, just . . .'

'You're not having it!' Bradey snapped. 'We're going back to the chalet.'

Maggie giggled.

'Yes, my master,' she said, and getting to her feet, she manoeuvred Bradey's wheel-chair away from the table.

The assistant *maître d'* came up swiftly.

'May I help?'

'You may not!' Bradey snapped. 'Good night to you!'

Watched by most diners, Maggie wheeled the chair past the Warrentons' table where Maria was regarding a silver bowl of caviar, set in crushed ice, as if it was something a cat had brought in, then, sighing, Maggie moved the chair into the lobby, down the gentle sloping ramp to their chalet.

'Caviar!' she moaned. 'I've never ever tasted it!'

'Then save up your money,' Bradey said, 'and have yourself a ball!'

'Honey, you seem in a bad mood.'

'I'm thinking! Be quiet!'

Back in the chalet with the curtains drawn, Bradey left the wheel-chair, poured himself a stiff Scotch and sat down in a comfortable arm-chair.

'Maggie! Business! Get out of that uniform, put on a simple dress and begin collecting information. Locate Mike. I want to talk to him.'

Ten minutes later, Maggie, now in a close-fitting blue dress that set off her figure to perfection left the chalet.

Twenty minutes crawled by while Bradey waited and thought, then Mike came in, still wearing his chauffeur's uniform.

Bradey regarded him. This was a man, he thought, not of Bradey's world: a tough, disciplined soldier and Bradey was surprised to realize he envied him.

'Come on in, Mike. Make yourself a drink.' He waved to the bottles on the table.

'No, thanks.' Mike closed the door and took a chair opposite where Bradey was sitting. 'Maggie said you wanted me.'

'How are you settling in?'

'Okay. The facilities for the staff are good. At the far end of the park there is a staff restaurant. The food is good. I've just had dinner there. I took my place next to one of the security guards who had come off duty. He spotted I'd been in the army. His name is Dave Putnam, an ex-sergeant like me. He's the talkative type. The other security guard was leaving when I arrived. He is older than Putnam who has no time for him. They don't get along together. Putnam was glad to have me for company.'

'Fine,' Bradey said. 'Keep him talking, Mike. I want to know about a couple I saw in the restaurant: Mr. and Mrs. Warrenton. She was wearing diamonds that will fetch a big price. See if you can find out if she hands over the diamonds to the guards for safe-keeping when she goes to bed. Don't rush it, Mike. We have a few days. Just keep this guy talking, then edge in the Warrentons. Say your boss knows them. I want you to take a long look at the two house dicks. From what I hear, they are tough cookies.'

Mike nodded. The pain in his side was nagging him.

'Okay. Putnam said he would be around later tonight. I'll have another word with him.' He got to his feet, controlling a grimace of pain. 'I'll get me some fresh air. See you,' and he walked to the door.

Bradey watched him leave. He felt a sudden unease. Was there something wrong with this big, tough-looking soldier? he wondered. Those sunken eyes, the tight, yellowish skin, and he had spotted sweat beads on Mike's forehead.

Maybe it was a slight fever. He knew Mike had been in Vietnam. Some minor thing that would pass.

Bradey rubbed the back of his head, frowning, then his mind shifted to the Warrenton diamonds.

* * *

Closing the cabin door, Manuel Torres pushed aside
the table and lifted the trap door. He reached down and
helped Fuentes out of the fish-smelling hole.

Fuentes was shaking with fright.

'What happened?'

'I bluffed them,' Manuel said, 'but not for long. Can you
swim?'

Fuentes' eyes opened wide.

'Swim? Yes.'

'Maybe you'll have to. That cop is tough. I know of him.
Wait,' and Manuel turned off the light. He left the cabin
like a shadow. Hiding behind the mast, he was able to
look down on the quay.

Detective Jacoby was sitting on a bollard, smoking a
cigarette. He was looking directly at the fishing vessel,
and Manuel nodded to himself. Unseen, he returned to
the cabin.

'You swim, my friend,' he said. 'They'll have a search-
warrant within an hour, and they'll crawl all over my
boat.'

'Swim where?' Fuentes asked, his voice husky.

'No distance. The third boat on the port side. The
owner is a good friend of mine. You tell him I sent you.
Then when you see my cabin light go out, you return. No
problem.'

After Lepski's telephone call, it took Beigler more than
an hour to obtain a search-warrant and to send two
detectives down to Manuel's fishing vessel. As Manuel
had anticipated, the boat was thoroughly searched. If
Fuentes had been on board, he would have been discovered.

Manuel gave Lepski a sly smile when the search ended.

'I hope now, Mr. Cop, you are satisfied that I am a man
of truth,' he said. 'My good friend, Fuentes, is happy with
his family in Havana.'

Lepski glared at him and stamped down the gang-plank.

Manuel stood on deck and watched the four detectives walk to their cars. When they had driven away, he returned to his cabin and turned off the light.

Half an hour later, he helped Fuentes climb aboard.

'They won't bother us again,' Manuel said. 'Get dry and sleep.'

* * *

Just after midnight, the feverish activities in the kitchens of the Spanish Bay Hotel came gradually to a halt. The chef and the second chef had gone home. The last meals had been served. Only the third chef remained. He would be on duty until 05.30, ready to prepare a meal for the few, returning from nightclubs or the casino, who demanded eggs and ham, scrambled eggs and sausages, grilled steaks and coffee.

At 01.30, the dishwashers and the cleaners had gone home, leaving the kitchens immaculate. The third chef and two waiters remained to pander to the pampered.

The third chef was Dominic Dezel. He was thirty years of age. Dark, not without good looks, his short stature irked him. More than anything else, he wished he'd been born like his brother, a chef now working at a two-star restaurant in Paris. His brother took after the father who was a giant of a man, whereas Dominic took after the mother who was almost a dwarf.

Dominic had been the sauce chef at one of the Relais hotels in France. Dulac, on vacation, and looking for talent, had been impressed by the sauce that was served with his *riz de veau* and scampi. He had talked to Dominic, and had persuaded him to come to the Spanish Bay Hotel as third chef.

The pay and the living conditions had been impressive, and Dominic was happy to reign over the kitchen from midnight to 05.30. It wasn't often, at these hours, his services were required. He spent the time in the chef's office, reading cook books and planning to open his own restaurant when he had accumulated enough capital. From time to time, there was a telephone call and he would hurry into the kitchens to prepare a meal.

The night was quiet. The two waiters were dozing in the still-room, away from the chef's office. Dominic, his feet on the chef's desk, was thinking about France, thinking of his family and planning to return when he had saved enough money.

The time was 02.30. Anita Certes came into the kitchens like a ghost. Bare-footed, silent, she closed the door, then paused.

When she had finished her evening duties, preparing the penthouse suite, she had concealed herself in the women's rest room in the basement of the hotel. Down the corridor from this rest room were the kitchens. She had locked herself in a toilet and sitting on the lid of the toilet, she had waited and waited. At 02.25, she came silently from the rest room and listened. The hotel was silent. She thought of the night detective who patrolled the hotel. He could be anywhere.

This man, Josh Prescott, frightened her. An ex-policeman, he took his job, protecting the hotel, seriously. She knew that from what the staff had told her. He had stopped a lot of pilfering, and the staff hated him. He wasn't the usual hotel dick who sat around, smoking and waiting for action. Josh Prescott was constantly on the prowl, looking for action. During the night, he walked the corridors, moved around the deserted restaurants, looked into the kitchens and even inspected the terraces and swimming-pools. He was here, there and everywhere: a big, bulky man with sandy hair and the bleak eyes of a dedicated cop.

Anita stood listening, looking around the dimly lit expanse of kitchens, at the stoves, the ovens, the glittering copper pots and pans hanging on the walls, the sinks, the big dish-washing machines. Where would it be safe to hide a bomb? For some minutes, standing just inside the kitchens, her back against the entrance door, she looked, wondered, then looked again.

No place she could see offered a *safe* hiding place. Her heart pounding, she moved across the expanse of floor to the store room where jars of stock lined the shelves, and bins, cheeses and the butter refrigerator stood against the wall. Here, possibly, could be a hiding place. She lifted the lid of a bin marked *FLOUR*. There must be half a hundred weight of flour in the bin, she thought. As she was staring down at the smooth white surface of the flour, she heard someone crossing the kitchens and coming to the store room. Hurriedly closing the lid of the bin, she looked wildly around for a place to hide, but there was nowhere. Was it Prescott? Her mind flew to Pedro. If Prescott found her here, she would be sacked!

She might even land in jail! Then there would be no way to get Pedro released!

Bracing herself, she moved out of the store room and found Dominic gaping at her.

'Anita! What are you doing here?' he asked.

She forced a smile and moved towards him.

'I am looking for you,' she said.

For sometime, Dominic had lusted for this squatly built, big-eyed Cuban girl. Every so often, she had allowed him to put his hand up her skirt in return for left-over food which she had told him was for her out-of-work husband. Her round, firm buttocks excited him. He had spent many hours, thinking of the moment when he would take her. Now, here she was at 02.30, telling him she was looking for him. So great was his lust for her, he didn't even wonder what she was doing in the hotel at this hour. All he could think of was she was looking for him, and that could mean only one thing.

He caught hold of her, pulling her against him. His hands slid down her back. Lifting her skirt, his fingers gripped her tight buttocks.

Anita closed her eyes. His fingers, gripping her flesh,

made her feel sick. She thought: 'Pedro, my darling, this is for you. Forgive me! This, what is happening, is for you.'

'Come to the office,' Dominic said, his voice strangled. 'It will be all right. We will make wonderful love.'

Putting his arm around her, he led her across the kitchens and to the chef's office. As she went with him, Anita was confident she had found a safe hiding place for the bomb. Now, she had to handle this man, giving him a little, but only a little.

They entered the office and Dominic closed the door.

'Lie over the desk. We must hurry,' he said.

Anita broke away from him.

'No! Not that way!'

Dominic, sweating, his heart hammering, stared at her.

'Lie over the desk! I know you want me! It's the only quick way. Lie over the desk!'

'No! We must find a bed,' Anita said, waving him away.

As Dominic began to expostulate, the telephone on the desk began to ring.

The sound of the bell was like a blow in Dominic's face. His lust vanished. He realized what he was doing. By this stupid act, he might ruin his career! He stared at Anita, now seeing her as a dark, not very attractive Cuban, and Cubans were as nothing to him. He must have been out of his mind to have lusted after this girl who was backing away, her eyes frightened.

He snatched up the telephone receiver.

'Scrambled eggs, sausages and coffee for two,' a man's voice snapped. The slur in his voice told Dominic he was drunk. 'Suite seven,' and the receiver was slammed down.

Dominic waved to a door at the far end of the office.

'Go that way! Quick!' and he hurried out of the office.

Shaking and thankful she wouldn't have to submit to this man's lust, Anita opened the door and found herself on a concrete path that led to the staff restaurant. She knew her way: a short cut, taking her behind the row of chalets, to the main road to Seacomb.

Holding her shoes in her hand, she ran silently into the darkness.

* * *

Two days passed.

During those days, the police continued their hunt for Fuentes, and finally decided he was indeed in Havana.

Pedro Certes, in intensive care ward, remained unconscious. A bored detective sat at his bedside.

Anita had been in touch with Manuel Torres. She went about her usual duties at the hotel. Manuel had warned her to keep away from his fishing vessel. They had met, the previous evening, at a small bar on the waterfront. She had told him the bomb could be hidden in the flour bin, and after thinking, Manuel had nodded approvingly. The two bombs hadn't arrived, but Manuel had heard from his friend, and the bombs would be arriving the following day. Manuel had assured her Pedro was surviving.

During these two days, both Maggie and Mike had been partially successful in obtaining the information Bradey needed. He decided he must talk to Ed Haddon who was staying at the Belleview Hotel, the second best hotel in the City.

A meeting was arranged. Haddon had reserved a table at a quiet, expensive sea-food restaurant near the yacht club.

Bradey had left his chalet at 21.00, stripped of his old man's disguise. He wore a business suit and a hat. At this hour, the Spanish Bay Hotel was busy. Bradey had no fears that anyone would notice him leaving the chalet. He walked briskly down the path that led to a taxi rank.

He found Haddon sitting at a secluded table, nibbling black olives with a double martini in front of him.

The two men greeted each other, and Haddon got Bradey a drink. The *maître d'* arrived with the menus.

'Have the chowder,' Haddon said. 'It's good.'

They ordered the clam chowder, then when the *maître d'* had gone away, Haddon asked, 'How's it taking shape?'

Bradey sipped his Scotch on the rocks, then reached for a black olive.

'Maggie is making progress. She has the reception clerk feeding out of her hand. The problem is to find the hotel safe. I've told her not to rush it. The reception clerk will eventually tell her, but we have to move cautiously. The opposition is tough. Mike has been circulating. He is now on friendly terms with one of the security guards. The second guard is tricky. The two house dicks are professionals. Mike has contacted them. He tells me they have to be handled with great care. The night dick is always looking for trouble.'

The waiter served the clam chowder. Both men began to eat. Haddon said, 'From what you're saying, Lu, it doesn't seem to me you're making much progress. I'm financing this deal. Every goddamn day you stay at the hotel is costing me money.'

Bradey hoisted a piece of clam into his mouth.

'You don't have to tell me. Ed. When I see what it is costing, my heart bleeds for you.' He grinned. 'But remember, what you put in, you take out.'

Haddon scowled at him.

'What's that supposed to mean?'

Bradey shovelled more food into his mouth, chewed and nodded approval.

'This swill is pretty good, Ed.'

'Cut this goddamn crap!' Haddon snarled. 'Have you something or haven't you?'

'Of course I have.' Bradey shovelled more food into his mouth. 'Does the name Silas Warrenton strike a bell?'

Haddon's eyes half closed.

'Who doesn't know of Silas Warrenton? What are you yammering about?'

Bradey went on eating. He kept Haddon waiting for some minutes before he laid down his fork.

'Warrenton's son, plus his newly wedded wife, are spending their honeymoon at the hotel's penthouse. She is plastered with diamonds.'

Haddon dropped his fork onto his plate.

'The Warrentons are at the Spanish Bay?'

Bradey grinned.

'That's what I'm telling you, Ed. She with her diamonds.'

Haddon pushed his plate aside. He was no longer interested in eating.

'Those diamonds, Lu, in the open market are worth at least eight million,' he said. 'A collar, bracelets and ear-rings. Right?'

Bradey nodded.

'That's what she was wearing when she came into the restaurant.'

'I've had my eye on those diamonds ever since I heard that rich old fool Gomez, her father, had bought them as a wedding present. He was taken to the cleaners. I hear he paid ten million. They are matched stones: something unique, but not worth ten.' Haddon eyed Bradey. 'So she was there with the diamonds. Go on.'

'The Warrentons are staying at the hotel for another ten days.' Bradey paused to eat, then went on, 'Now, look, Ed, I know the original idea was to bust the hotel's safe and we would pick up around five million. It looked good to me, but so far, I haven't been able to locate the safe. I know the opposition is fierce: security guards and house dicks. I'm beginning to wonder if we would be safer off going after the Warrentons' diamonds and forget the safe.'

Haddon began to toy with the chowder again.

'Keep talking, Lu,' he said. 'I hear you.'

'When you steered Mike Bannion to me, you picked a smart guy,' Bradey said. 'He's not only a dead shot, but he has that thing ex-army men have.' He shook his head. 'I envy him. Take one look at him and you think this is a guy

you can trust.' He paused to eat again. 'But he worries
me, Ed. I keep wondering why a guy like him should turn
crooked. It doesn't make sense to me.'

Haddon made an impatient movement.

'Why bring him up? His brother who is more crooked
than you are, and that's saying a lot, guarantees this guy,
and that's good enough for me. Why make complications?
Are you telling me you're not satisfied with Mike Bannion's performance?'

'No. He's almost too good to be true. I'm not saying
that. He just puzzles me, and another thing, I don't like
the way he looks. He looks like a sick man.'

Haddon shrugged.

'His brother told me Mike badly needs money. So,
okay, if he delivers, why should you care?'

Bradey finished the chowder.

'I guess you have a point.'

'How the hell did we get into this? I'm not interested in
Bannion. I'm interested in the diamonds.'

'I've been working on this. I put Mike in the photo and
last night he came up with the info I wanted. What I
wanted to know was if this Warrenton woman put her
diamonds in safe custody every night. That is, if she uses
the box the hotel supplies for every client, and this box is
locked in the hotel safe. The security guard told Mike she
doesn't. She is one of those arrogant bitches who think,
because she lives in the hotel, her jewels are safe, and she
can't be bothered to hand them over, get a receipt from
the guard after a late night out. The security guard told
Mike that there was quite a scene when this guard warned
her she was taking a risk. He pointed out the hotel would
take no responsibility if her jewels were stolen. She told
him to go to hell. Then Dulac called on her, again
pointing out the risk. She told him it was his business to
make the penthouse secure. This he has done. You want
service at the Spanish Bay Hotel, you get it.' Bradey
paused, then went on, 'So a concealed safe has been
installed. Both Dulac and the Warrenton woman imagine

her diamonds are safe.' Bradey grinned. 'Safes? They're jokes to me. I can get those diamonds, Ed, if you are interested.'

Haddon signalled to the *maître d'* who hurried to the table.

'Pecan pie,' Haddon said. 'Okay with you?'

'Me, apple pie,' Bradey said and sat back to pick his teeth.

He watched Haddon staring down at the table cloth. He knew Haddon's mind was busy so he kept quiet. When the pies were served, Haddon said, 'The problem will be to dispose of the diamonds, but I think it can be arranged. The one man who can handle a deal like this is Claude Kendrick. I'll talk to him tomorrow.'

Bradey attacked his apple pie. He was pleased that Haddon hadn't even queried his ability to get the diamonds.

Haddon ate his pie slowly, his eyebrows down in a frown of concentration. Bradey, knowing the signs, relaxed and enjoyed his pie.

The pies finished, coffee was served with balloon glasses of brandy.

Haddon said abruptly, 'You wondered if we would be safer going after the Warrenton's diamonds than busting the hotel safe.'

Bradey looked sharply at him.

'Makes sense, doesn't it?'

'Most things you say, Lu, make sense,' Haddon said quietly. 'Your trouble is you don't think big.'

'Eight million seems big to me,' Bradey said with a sly smile.

'Thirteen million, possibly fifteen million looks bigger, doesn't it?'

Bradey sipped his brandy.

'You mean we grab the diamonds as well as busting the hotel safe?'

'I'm not saying we will do it, but let's take a long hard look at it. Find out where the safe is located. Then when you have found that out, we'll talk again. In the meantime, I'll talk to Kendrick about the Warrenton's diamonds. Let's get a hustle on, Lu. Suppose we meet here tomorrow night at the same time? I'll have news for you: you have news for me. Right?'

Bradey hesitated, then nodded.

'I'll talk to Maggie,' he said, shook hands and leaving Haddon to settle the bill, he hurried out into the humid night.

* * *

During the past hour, Maggie had been talking to Mike Bannion. They were seated in the comfortable lounge of the chalet, both having had dinner in the staff restaurant.

Maggie had taken a liking to Mike. He reminded her of her father who had been an army sergeant before being dishonourably discharged for large-scale pilfering. Now dead, killed in a brawl, Maggie often thought of him. When he wasn't drunk, he had been devoted to Maggie, and she to him. She had had no time for her mother, and when her father was killed, her one thought was to leave home. At the age of thirteen, she had seduced the headmaster of her school. He had gone to jail, and she had been put 'into care'. Escaping, she was taken up by a rich old roué who was partial to young girls. She learned a lot from him: her sexual technique became impressive. Six years as a call girl hadn't spoilt nor toughened her. She was, Bradey had often thought, the blue-print of a whore with a golden heart.

She had a warm, sympathetic streak in her that men could sense. She was used to men confiding their troubles to her, and she always listened, patted them, smiled at them and let them unburden.

It wasn't long before Mike told her about his daughter, Chrissy. They had been sitting together, waiting for Bradey to return from his meeting with Haddon, and Maggie had told Mike about her father.

'You remind me of him,' she said. 'Not in looks, but by the way you talk. Soldiers talk alike.'

'I guess,' Mike said. 'You know, Maggie, I have never done a crooked thing in my life until now.'

Maggie laughed.

'I've wondered about that. I'm not crazy about this business, but I'm crazy about Lu. I would do anything for him. What made you join with us, Mike?'

So he told her about Chrissy. Listening, Maggie became so moved, tears came to her eyes.

'How awful!' she exclaimed when Mike had explained that the money Bradey was going to pay him would go to take care of Chrissy until she died. 'You mean the poor little thing will die in fifteen years time?'

Mike nodded.

'Why, that's terrible!' Maggie wiped a tear away. 'Mike, you are a marvellous father!'

'I love her,' Mike said quietly. 'My one thought is to provide for her. That's the only reason why I'm doing this job.' He looked at Maggie. 'Will it work?'

'It'll work,' Maggie said. 'Lu is marvellous! You don't think I want to go to jail?' She grimaced. 'What a thought! But Lu told me it will work and I won't go to jail, so that means it will work, Mike. Don't worry about that.'

'Lu isn't really an old man, is he? When he leaves his wheel-chair, his movements are those of a young man.'

'He's younger than you are, Mike. He is a great artist. Don't worry.'

At this moment, they heard Bradey enter the chalet and walk quickly to the bedroom, he and Maggie shared.

As he passed the living-room door, he called, 'Maggie! I want you!'

Maggie scrambled to her feet and ran into the bedroom, shutting the door. Bradey was sitting at the dressing-table, quickly putting on his disguise. He had no intention of letting Mike see what he really looked like. He was uneasy about Mike. If something went wrong and Mike got into the hands of the police, he just might give them a description of Bradey as he really was, and that must never happen.

'Hi, darling,' Maggie exclaimed, coming to him.

He waved her away, intent on turning himself into an old man.

'Baby! Work! This reception clerk, Claude Previn. How's it going with him?'

There was a snap in his voice that startled Maggie.

'Is something wrong, honey?'

'Don't yammer,' Bradey said, fixing his moustache. 'How are you and Previn progressing?'

'He's so hot he's likely to burst into flames,' Maggie said.

'He's off duty now?'

'Yes.'

'Can you contact him?'

Maggie blinked.

'You mean *now*?'

'Of course I mean now! Don't be a pea-brain!'

'Oh, Lu, you do sound cross!' Maggie said. 'I don't know if I can contact him. I do have his telephone number.'

'Where does he live?'

'He didn't tell me.'

Bradey gave an exasperated sigh.

'Call him!' He finished fixing his moustache, and began working age into the skin on his face. 'Now pay attention. You are going to him, wherever he is, and you're going to screw him stupid. Understand? When you have softened him up, you are going to find out where the hotel safe is located.'

Maggie's eyes opened wide.

'How do I do that, hon?'

'Tell him your patient is eccentric. He's expecting some valuable jewellery which he plans to give his daughter. He wants to know about the security system of the hotel, and where the safe is. He will want to inspect the safe. Tell him you are scared of your patient and you don't want

94

to lose your job. Tell him your patient is very difficult. Are you with me?'

Maggie thought for a long moment. Bradey could almost hear her brain working.

'But, Lu, pet, can't I tell him all this tomorrow when he's on duty, instead of having to go to bed with him?'

'No! When we bust the safe, the cops will ask questions. I don't want you to be involved. Previn will keep his mouth shut rather than admit he has been having it off with you.'

Maggie considered this, then she smiled.

'I always thought you were smart, Lu.'

Bradey pointed to the telephone.

'Call him.'

* * *

The following evening, Ed Haddon was sitting at the corner table of the sea-food restaurant, nibbling black olives, a double martini before him when Bradey came in.

The *maître d'* arrived as Bradey sat down.

'Have the Chicken Maryland,' Haddon said. 'It's good.'

Bradey said the Chicken Maryland was fine with him. Haddon ordered a Scotch on the rocks for Bradey which arrived while the two men sat silently waiting.

After Bradey had sipped his drink, he said, 'You asked for action, Ed. You've got it.'

'No more than I expected.' Haddon grinned. 'As partners, we're the best.'

As the waiter was fussing around, providing bread rolls, butter and *canapés*, the two men relapsed into silence. It wasn't until the chicken was served and the waiter had gone, Haddon said, 'You found out where the safe is?'

Bradey cut off a portion of chicken breast, dipped it into a bowl of chilli sauce and conveyed it to his mouth. He chewed, nodded, said, 'This is great!'

Haddon had never known anyone as devoted to food as Bradey. In spite of his leanness, Bradey adored good cooking. Haddon contained his impatience. After five minutes while Bradey ate as if he hadn't eaten for a week, Haddon repeated his question.

'The safe?'

'Gimme a minute,' Bradey said, cutting into the chicken thigh. 'You know something, Ed?' He was speaking with his mouth full. 'When I was a kid, I starved. I'm not kidding. If I got a bit of mouldy bread once a day, I was lucky. My mum died of starvation. Food is the most beautiful thing in life!'

Haddon lost patience.

'Lu! The goddamn safe!' The rasp in his voice startled Bradey who reluctantly laid down his fork.

'Maggie got the dope. You'll never guess where the hotel safe is located. You would have thought it was somewhere behind the reception desk where most safes are or even in the basement. Right?'

Haddon snarled, 'Where is it?'

'On the penthouse floor. How do you like that?'

Haddon absorbed this information, then grinned.

'I love it. Tell me.'

'Maggie got the reception clerk to bed. She spun him a yarn about her eccentric patient. Maggie really knows her business, and Previn was drained dry. So she fixed he should conduct me with Maggie to take a look at the safe. There's a special elevator up to the penthouse floor that leads right into the safe room. The Warrentons wouldn't even know the safe room is up there. What happens is this: every night, before the guests retire, they call the security guards and put their valuables into boxes: each box is numbered and the guests get a receipt. The boxes are taken by this elevator to the safe. This service begins at 23.00 to 02.00. After that time, the service packs up. Previn—the reception clerk—panting to get Maggie into his bed again, gave me a look-see. This is strictly against hotel regulations, but Maggie sexed him with promises of yet another night. The safe looks tough, but that's my business. What the real problem is, once we bust the safe, is how to get all those boxes down from the penthouse floor and out of the hotel. This needs thought.'

Haddon nodded.

'I'll give it thought too.' He ate while he brooded, then he went on, 'I've seen Kendrick. He can handle the Warrenton diamonds. He offers five million. That means he will get six. Fair enough. But he is uneasy about the boxes. They will have to be opened and the lot valued. This will take time. The heat will be fierce. The first suspect will be Kendrick. I can see his angle. Maybe I'll have to find another fence for the boxes.'

Bradey grimaced.

'Maybe it would be better to forget the boxes and go for the Warrenton diamonds.'

'If the safe had been anywhere else but on the penthouse floor, Lu, I would agree with you, but this is like a gift from the gods. All this needs is more thought. The Warrentons' diamonds, plus the contents of the boxes, will give us *each* something like eight million.'

Bradey considered this. Eight million! What couldn't he do with a sum like that!

'Tell me about the safe room and this elevator,' Haddon went on, watching the greed lighting up in Bradey's eyes.

'The elevator is located on the top floor, then goes up, one floor, to the penthouse floor. The elevator door on the top flood is concealed by a door marked *Service*. Previn unlocked this door and Maggie pushed my chair into the cage. There is a lock, instead of a button, on the elevator. Previn had a key. Putting the key in the lock and turning the key, caused the elevator to rise up one floor and we moved into the safe room. This room has no windows nor doors, but I saw there was a trap door in the ceiling which was probably a way of escape, onto the roof, in case of fire.'

Haddon finished his chicken.

'Okay, Lu, think about it. Did you get a look at one of the security boxes?'

'Sure. Previn showed me one. The lock is for the birds.'

'If there were twenty boxes in that safe, how long would it take you to open all of them?'

'Half an hour,' Bradey replied promptly.

'So, suppose, after you have grabbed the Warrentons' diamonds, you get into the safe room, open the safe, open the boxes, empty their contents into a sack, close the boxes, put them back and relock the safe. Suppose you did that?'

Bradey turned this suggestion over in his mind.

'It'll need thought and organizing, Ed, but it's an idea. Give me a day or so to think about it, will you?'

'I'll have to talk to Kendrick again,' Haddon said. 'Yes, the night after tomorrow. We'll get this finalized. Right?'

'The night after tomorrow here,' Bradey said, then, 'How about some of that apple pie I had the other night? It was good.'

Five

As the sun, like a crimson rim of fire, slid into the sea and
dusk settled over the waterfront, Manuel Torres walked
towards his fishing vessel. He carried a canvas sack over
his shoulder. His bald head resembled an orange in the
light of the fading sunset.

He paused now and then to exchange greetings with
other Cubans who were aimlessly waiting for the time
when they could return to their shacks, hoping their
wives would provide some sort of meal.

There was a cold, gloomy expression on Manuel's face
as he walked the gang-plank onto his vessel. Carefully, he
laid down the canvas sack, then pulled in the gang-plank.
As he had approached his vessel, his eyes darted to right
and left. There were no signs of watching detectives, nor
even a cop.

He whistled to alert Fuentes that he was back, then
picking up the sack, he walked the deck to the forward
cabin which was in darkness. He had warned Fuentes not
to put on the lights. He had been away some six hours,
and he felt sorry for Fuentes, sitting in the growing
darkness, alone, but at least he had left him food.

He entered the cabin, closed the door, then turned on
the light.

Fuentes, lying on the bunk, sat up.

'You have taken your time!' he snarled. 'Do you imagine I like it, lying here, waiting and waiting?'

'My friend,' Manuel said quietly, 'you have no need to wait and wait. You are not a prisoner. You have only to get up and walk away. No one, except the cops, will stop you.'

Deflated, Fuentes lay back on the hard mattress.

'I'm worked up. It is no fun being cooped up in this hot cabin for hours. Forget it, Manuel. I know you are doing your best for me, and I'm grateful.'

Manuel began to unpack the canvas sack.

'Tonight, we will eat well,' he said. 'Pasta, chicken, cheese.'

Fuentes was studying Manuel's face, lit by the overhead lamp. Manuel's dark, brooding expression alarmed him.

'Is there something wrong?' he asked. He got off the bunk and approached the table on which Manuel was laying out a pack of spaghetti, cans of tomato and chilli sauces and a plump chicken.

'We eat first,' Manuel said. 'I am hungry.'

Although he hadn't emptied the sack, he pulled the strings, closing the sack and placed it carefully in a locker.

'You have something else there?' Fuentes asked.

'The bombs,' Manuel said. 'But first we eat.'

He moved into the small galley. After putting a saucepan of water on the gas ring, then turning on the electric grill, he opened the cans. He put the chicken on the rotor spit. His movements were methodical: his expression remained gloomy.

Fuentes stood in the doorway of the galley, nervously watching Manuel. He hadn't seen this man so thoughtful nor so gloomy before, and his nervousness increased.

'Is there trouble?' he asked after some minutes.

'We eat. Then we talk,' Manuel said, putting the spaghetti into the now boiling water.

Fuentes returned to the cabin and set knives and forks. He then sat on the bunk and waited.

Forty minutes later, the two men sat at the table, each with half a grilled chicken and a bowl of spaghetti, smothered in chilli and tomato sauces.

Manuel wolfed down the food. His face was still set in a gloomy mask. Fuentes, uneasy, ate slowly. He kept looking at Manuel, then away.

Finally, he exploded, 'Manuel, my friend! What has happened? Tell me for the love of God!'

'He is going to die,' Manuel said, finishing the last of the chicken.

Fuentes stiffened.

'You mean Pedro?'

'Who else? I have talked to my friend at the hospital. There is now no hope. It is a matter of time. Pedro could survive for a week, even two weeks, but he is a dead man already.'

Fuentes, who thought only of himself, relaxed.

'So we don't need the bombs?' He had a horror of being connected with bombs. 'So we have less problems?'

Manuel stared at him. His little eyes were like black olives.

'My friend, you are not thinking. You seem to have forgotten what we are planning to do: you, Anita and me.'

Fuentes stared at him.

'You are wrong! I know well what we plan to do! We get into the penthouse of the hotel, hold these two rich people to ransom and leave for Havana with five million dollars. Why do you say I am not thinking?'

'How do we get into the penthouse?'

Fuentes flung up his hands in a gesture of impatience.

'This has been arranged. Anita has a duplicate pass-key. She will get us into the penthouse. Why are you saying I am not thinking?'

'Now, you are not only not thinking, my friend, but you are not remembering,' Manuel said, cutting himself a piece of cheese. 'You have forgotten Anita promised to get us into the penthouse on one condition.' He leaned forward, staring at Fuentes. 'Pedro is to be released and travel with us to Havana.'

Fuentes ran his fingers through his long, greasy hair.

'But you tell me he is dying.'

101

'Now, my friend, you are beginning to see the problem. Yes, Pedro will be dead in a week or so. Anita loves this man. She is ready to do anything to get him back with her.' Manuel cut himself another piece of cheese. 'Women need understanding. I understand them. Money means nothing to her. Her life is bound up with Pedro. I have given my word to her that if she gets us into the penthouse, her man will be released and will go with us to Havana. I have done everything possible to make Pedro's release certain. I have two bombs that will create such pressure, Pedro will be released.' He shut his eyes and Fuentes could see he was in torment.

There was a long silence while Fuentes watched Manuel with growing impatience, but this big man scared him, so he kept silent.

'I gave my word to Anita,' Manuel went on, staring down at his big hands, resting on the table. 'I promised her I would get her husband released if she would get us into the penthouse. That was the bargain.'

'I know,' Fuentes said, 'but Pedro is dying.'

'Yes. That is without doubt. So there is no bargain between Anita and myself.'

Fuentes clutched his head in his hands.

'Are you telling me we are going to lose five million dollars because this stupid woman who is so besotted with this useless creep, won't get us into the penthouse if she knows the bastard is dying?' Fuentes shouted.

'That is what I am telling you. A man like you wouldn't understand. I am known as a man of truth.' Manuel paused, staring into space, then he went on. 'Five million dollars are involved. It is said every man has his price.' Manuel wiped the sweat off his face. 'Five million dollars! I have suffered hours to come to a decision. Five million dollars! With that kind of money many doors that have stayed locked to me will open.'

'You are forgetting my share,' Fuentes said sharply.

Maneul's black, olive-like eyes were expressionless as he nodded.

'Yes. You get a million. So four million dollars!'

'What is your decision?' Fuentes asked, the muscles in his fat face twitching.

'I will have to lie to her. To lie to her reduces me in my own eyes. To have to lie to one of my people is an act of shame.' Manuel clenched his fists. 'You think only of money. That I can understand. You are a poor man. This lie that I will be forced to tell her will make a hole in my heart.'

With an effort, Fuentes kept control of himself. He wanted to scream at Manuel to stop acting like a goddamn ham. Who cared about Anita? What was she, anyway? A nothing, like her creep of a husband! But he restrained himself and remained silent. No one screamed at Manuel without his fist smashing into their faces.

'The bombs?' he asked, after a long silence. 'Will they be necessary now?'

'Of course. We will have to act out the lie. She is not stupid. I will have to lie to her with the greatest care.' He got to his feet. 'Go to bed, my friend. In half an hour, I meet Anita. We mustn't waste any more time. If Pedro dies tomorrow or the day after, Anita might learn of his death, then there will be no five millions. She must get us into the penthouse by the night after next.'

'We will need guns,' Fuentes said.

'All that is arranged. Everything is arranged except for Anita's part in the operation.'

Half an hour later, Manuel left his fishing vessel and walked along the waterfront, carrying the canvas sack that contained the two bombs. He reached Anita's walk-up apartment, climbed the stairs and knocked on her door.

Anita jerked the door open. In the harsh overhead light, Manuel thought she looked ill. There were dark patches under her eyes and she seemed to have shrunk.

'Good news,' Manuel said as he moved into the little living-room.

Anita's eyes lit up as she closed the door.

'Pedro?'

'Yes, Pedro.' Manuel placed the canvas sack on the table. His thick lips moved into a false smile. 'I have just come from the hospital. My friend there tells me Pedro has recovered consciousness, and his fever has abated. In another two days, it will be safe to move him.'

Anita stared at him.

'I can't believe it!' she whispered. 'He was so ill. In two days? No, it can't be possible!'

'Antibiotics work miracles,' Manuel said, trying to avoid Anita's searching stare. 'My friend at the hospital tells me the cops are already trying to question your husband. He is a fine lad, Anita! You should be proud of him! He refuses to tell them anything. Even now, they don't know who he is. He's protecting you.'

Anita's face crumpled. She turned away and ran into the tiny bedroom. Listening to her sobs, Manuel closed his eyes. Would four million dollars ever erase this moment when he could no longer call himself a man of truth?

He waited, sweat on his face, then as the sound of her sobs ceased, he moved silently to the door and peered into the bedroom.

Anita was on her knees, her head bowed in prayer, thanking God for this miracle, and Manuel, grimacing, turned away.

Ten minutes later, Anita came from the bedroom, looking a different woman. She had bathed her eyes, combed her hair, and her hard expression told Manuel she was now the woman he needed to get them into the penthouse.

'God has answered my prayers,' she said, catching hold of Manuel's right hand in both of hers. 'I have never ceased to pray. God has listened to me! Now, we must get Pedro home! In two days, you say he can travel?'

'Yes, but there are a number of things to arrange in these two days,' Manuel said. 'First the bombs.' He went to the table and opened the sack, producing a black box the size and shape of a cigarette packet. 'This is the little

104

bomb. You must conceal it in the hotel lobby.' He took another black box from the sack. This box was four times the size of the first box and wrapped in cellophane. He laid the box carefully on the table. 'This is the big bomb that will destroy the kitchens. I hope we don't have to use it.' Then he took a small box from the sack. 'This is the detonator. You see these two buttons. I press the top button and the small bomb explodes. I press the second button and the big bomb explodes. I will have this with me. You will have the two bombs.'

Anita moved forward and stared at the two boxes on the table. Manuel watched her. Her hard, determined expression gave him confidence.

'I will hide these bombs,' she said. 'You can rely on me.'

'Good,' Manuel said. 'Tomorrow night, Fuentes and I will come here at midnight. Then we three will go to the hotel. You are still sure you can get us into the penthouse?'

'I am sure,' Anita said.

'Then tomorrow night, here, at midnight.' Manuel moved to the door.

She put her hand on his arm.

'I trust you. You are a good man. I don't trust Fuentes, but you . . .' She stared directly at him. 'Our people say you are a man of truth. I do this only for Pedro.'

Manuel moved out into the corridor.

'All will be well,' he said, hating himself, but now only thinking what four million dollars would mean to his future. 'Tomorrow night,' and he walked down the corridor and down the stairs while Anita watched him.

She closed and locked the door, then she went across the room, opened a drawer and took from it a stabbing knife that Pedro kept, explaining to her that there were times when a man had to protect himself.

She pulled the knife from its sheaf. She thought of Josh Prescott, the hotel's night detective. He was the menace. He was the only one to prevent her hiding the bombs.

She regarded the glittering blade. For Pedro, she would do anything: even take a life.

She changed into a black sweat shirt and black trousers. She fastened the knife to her belt and pulled the sweat shirt down to conceal the knife. Then she put the two bombs in a plastic sack.

The time now was 01.15.

Leaving her room, she began the long walk to the Spanish Bay Hotel.

* * *

Every man has a weakness, and Josh Prescott, the night detective at the Spanish Bay Hotel, was no exception. He was a man of fixed routine. He was also a man who was over fond of women. Even he admitted that he was over-sexed.

Mike Bannion, knowing this man was dangerous, had studied his routine. At 01.00, Prescott patrolled the corridors of the hotel. At 01.40, he walked around the hotel lobby and the empty restaurants. At 02.00, he visited the kitchens. At 02.45 he patrolled the hotel grounds and the swimming-pool. He was so punctual, Mike could set a watch by this routine. This was Prescott's weakness. Bannion had passed this information on to Bradey.

So at 02.45, Maggie slid into the swimming-pool, now deserted, and in the bright overhead lights, she swam with the grace of a mermaid, and Prescott paused to stare.

He had caught sight of her from time to time and had considered her some doll, but standing on the edge of the swimming-pool, watching her cavort, practically naked in a mini-bikini, he, as Bradey knew he would, reacted strongly to her sexy charms.

Maggie, well versed, waved to him and swam to the steps. She made a pretence of not being able to climb the steps, and Prescott hurried forward, taking her hand.

Bradey, watching from the shadows, gave a nod of

approval. He moved silently and swiftly to the side entrance of the hotel, knowing Prescott would be fully occupied for at least half an hour.

Even at this hour, there were people in the lobby, most of them half drunk, saying noisy good-byes before they went up to their various suites.

Wearing a tuxedo, a carnation in his button-hole and a blond chin beard, Bradey walked without hesitation across the lobby to the elevators. No one paid him any attention. He was part of the background scene.

At this hour the elevators were on automatic. He entered one of the cages, pressed the top-floor button.

Four minutes later, he had unlocked the door marked *Service* and entered the elevator that would take him to the safe room.

It took him several minutes to adjust his implement to start the elevator. He was quite relaxed, knowing the two security guards, by now, had collected the jewels and valuables from those in the various suites, and had stowed them away in the security boxes and had locked the boxes in the safe.

Turning on the light, he examined the three locks of the safe. No problem there, he told himself. He would have to make and bend a piece of steel. These locks were for the birds. He was more interested in the fire-escape hatch in the ceiling.

Pulling the bolt and easing the trap-door to fall, he climbed the ladder and came out into the moonlit night. With cat-like silence, he edged forward and looked directly down on the penthouse terrace.

There, below, in dim lighting, were lounging chairs, several glass-topped tables and a splendid view of the beach and ocean.

Lights came from the penthouse. As he stood, watching, a shadow appeared, then Maria Warrenton wandered onto the terrace. She was naked, except for her diamonds.

Bradey regarded her, crouching now, his eyes only on

107

the glitter of the diamonds that lit up like fire in the moonlight.

Then Wilbur Warrenton came out onto the terrace. He carried a Nikon camera with a flash attachment.

While Maria posed against the penthouse railings, the moonlight directly on her, Wilbur photographed her.

Watching, Bradey thought he would like to see the prints. How these rich loved to show off! This woman had a good body, and her sun-tanned skin set off the glittering diamonds, but in spite of the diamonds, Bradey decided, she wasn't in Maggie's class.

'These will be fine,' Wilbur said. 'Now, let's go to bed.'

Bradey watched Maria as she moved away from the railings and went to Wilbur, putting her arms around him.

'We'll sleep late,' she said. 'Tired?'

'Well, it's been quite a day. These diamonds are marvellous on you, and you are even more marvellous.'

Together, they went into the penthouse and out of Bradey's sight.

He remained motionless until the lights went out. Then, in the moonlight, he swung himself silently from the roof onto the terrace.

The big glass doors of the penthouse were wide open and he smiled to himself. This was going to be a very easy job. He moved like a shadow into the big living-room.

Tossed carelessly on one of the settees were the diamonds. Bradey came to a halt, scarcely believing what he saw. A faint light came from the master bedroom, and he heard Maria release a moan.

'Yes, now, darling,' she exclaimed. 'Quickly . . . now!'

Bradey was tempted to snatch up this fortune in stones, but remembering Haddon also wanted the contents of the boxes in the safe, he turned away.

Tomorrow night! he thought. What a killing!

He swung himself up onto the roof of the penthouse and down into the safe room. Then getting into the elevator, he descended to the top floor. He relocked the

Service door, then satisfied, he took the elevator down to the first floor.

The time now was 02.50. Leaning over the staircase rail, he looked down into the hotel lobby. There were still a few people talking, but they were moving to the elevators.

Sure, Maggie was still keeping the hotel dick occupied, Bradey sauntered down the stairs. He looked like just another departing guest.

Five minutes later, he was back in his chalet. Twenty minutes later, Maggie joined him in their bedroom.

'Phew!' she exclaimed. 'He's quite a lover! We had it off in the shrubbery.'

Bradey, sitting on the bed, looked admiringly at her.

'What a girl! How about tomorrow night?'

She stripped off her bikini.

'We have a date.' She moved to the bathroom. 'He was just a little too keen. Mind if I sleep, hon? I'm truly flaked out.'

Bradey grinned.

'If ever a girl deserves her sleep you do,' he said. 'We do the job tomorrow night.'

'Honest?'

'Go take a shower. Tomorrow night.'

As he undressed, he thought of those diamonds, lying on the settee. Would that careless bitch throw them on the settee tomorrow night? Was it going to be that easy? He had a sudden cold feeling that he might have missed the opportunity of a lifetime.

* * *

Anita, in her black sweat shirt and black trousers, moved invisibly through the grounds of the Spanish Bay Hotel. She was heading for the staff entrance which meant she would have to circle the swimming-pool.

She paused, seeing Josh Prescott standing under the lights of the pool, and her heart skipped a beat. Then she

109

saw him helping Maggie out of the pool. She watched Maggie, sex oozing out of her. She watched them talk, then she watched Maggie catch hold of Prescott's arm and lead him away towards the flowering shrubs.

No longer frightened of being caught by Prescott, Anita ran swiftly to the staff entrance. With her duplicate pass-key, she let herself into the dark corridor and walked silently to the kitchens.

Opening the door, she peered in. She heard the clatter of crockery and cutlery and she guessed the two waiters were in the still-room, preparing the breakfast trays, but where was Dominic, the third chef?

She slid into the dimly lit kitchen and looked across to the lighted chef's office. She could see Dominic at the desk, reading.

Moving fast, she reached the store room. Lifting the lid of the flour bin, she used the scoop to make a deep hole in the flour. She inserted the big bomb, pushing it gently down and then, breathing heavily, her heart racing, she buried the bomb. Carefully, she smoothed over the surface of the flour, wiped her hands hastily on a towel by the bin, then moved swiftly out of the store room.

As she began the long walk across the kitchens, the telephone bell began to ring in the chef's office. She broke into a silent run, reached the door as one of the waiters came out of the still room. He didn't look her way, but hurried into the chef's office.

She heard Dominic call, 'Grilled ham and eggs for suite six . . .' and she was running down the corridor, out through the staff entrance door and into the humid night.

How long would Prescott be before he returned to the hotel?

She ran around the hotel and up the entrance steps. She paused to look around. The lobby was deserted. The night porter was out of sight. She moved into the lobby, looked wildly around for a hiding place for the little bomb. Across the lobby, she saw, on the wall, near the entrance

110

to the restaurant, a large painted wooden carving of a Mexican woman.

Jean Dulac had discovered this carving in a wayside village some miles from Taxco, Mexico. With his wide knowledge of antiques, he had recognized this carving to be of the Cortes period and had bought it. It now had pride of place in the lobby.

Anita ran over to it. Here, she found a crevice between the woman's breasts. The little bomb fitted into the crevice as if it were made for it.

A man's slurring voice said, 'A pretty thing, baby, but you are prettier.'

Anita's heart gave a bound, then raced. Her hand went to the hilt of her knife, concealed under her sweat shirt. She turned.

A fat, white-haired man was sitting in a deep lounging chair, watching her. His face was flushed and he looked half-asleep.

'Where did you spring from?' he asked.

Controlling her panic, Anita said, 'I'm just one of the cleaners.'

'Pretty. I guess I'll go to bed.' He levered himself out of the chair and came unsteadily towards her. She could see he was very drunk.

She slid around him and ran to the hotel's entrance.

'Hey! Don't run away,' the man exclaimed. 'How about a little kiss?'

But she was now down the steps and into the night, running as she had never run before. As she reached the entrance gates and began to run down the boulevard, she heard a voice she recognized.

'Anita!'

She paused, looking back.

A battered Lincoln pulled out of the shadows and stopped by her.

Manuel grinned at her.

'I've been waiting,' he said. 'Okay?'

'Yes.' She shuddered. 'I said I would do it. It is done!'

111

'Get in,' Manuel said, opening the passenger's door. 'You are a splendid woman!'

She ran around the car and scrambled in beside him.

'Pedro? Have you heard more news?' she asked.

Manuel patted her knee.

'I have just come from the hospital,' he lied. 'All goes wonderfully well. There is talk of moving your husband to the prison hospital the day after tomorrow. He refuses to tell them anything. He thinks only of you, and is protecting you. He is a fine young man as you are a fine young woman.'

'He is really so much better?'

'It is as I say. Now tell me about the bombs.'

As he drove her back to her home, Manuel listened to what she had done with the two bombs, her voice unsteady, tears of relief running down her face. He listened, nodding approval, and yet there was in him this sick feeling that he was betraying her.

But he kept thinking: five million dollars! What couldn't he do with a sum like that! He also thought of Fuentes. To give such a hollow, worthless man a million would be absurd! No, five million was always better than four million. When the time came, he would get rid of Fuentes: a quick blow and then the sea. It would be simple.

As he pulled up outside Anita's apartment block, he patted her arm.

'We do this tomorrow night. We will come here and finalize our plans at midnight. Okay?'

She caught hold of his hand in both of hers.

'Yes. Tomorrow night.' She paused, then went on, 'My friend, I trust you. You are known as a man of truth. Money means nothing to me. All I want is Pedro, my husband. I trust you.'

Sour bile rose in Manuel's mouth. He swallowed, grimacing as he again patted her arm.

'Rely on me,' he said, unable to look directly at her.

'You will have your husband. Tomorrow night, then, at midnight.'

'May God bless and keep you,' she said, and lifting his hand, she pressed her lips against his hard, scaly skin.

'Go to bed,' he said, snatching his hand away. 'Tomorrow night.'

He watched her walk up the steps to the entrance of her home. She was again crying.

With a shiver, he wiped the back of his hand, wiping away the touch of her lips. For a long moment, he sat staring through the dusty windshield of his car, hating himself, then with the thought of owning five million dollars, he lifted his heavy shoulders in a despairing shrug, shifted into gear and drove away.

* * *

The following morning, in the air-conditioned living-room of the hotel chalet, Lu Bradey sat in the wheel-chair in his disguise of an old man, shaping a small strip of steel with the aid of a file.

Across the room, Mike Bannion watched him.

Maggie had gone for a swim in the pool. She had told Bradey, the previous night, about Mike's daughter, Chrissy, and because he had come to like this big ex-Army sergeant, Bradey had been shocked.

A long silence had dwelt over the room except for the faint rasping sound of the file. From time to time, Bradey had taken a swift glance at Mike, then away.

Breaking the silence, Mike said, 'You know your job. What is that for?'

Bradey put down the file and flexed his fingers.

'This bit of steel, Mike, will open the safe.' He nodded. 'I guess I do know my job.' He paused to light a cigarette. 'Tonight, we do the job. It should be easy. Maggie told me about your little daughter. I'm sorry. You will get the money, Mike. With luck, this job will be no problem. Does it worry you?'

113

Mike shook his head.

'No. If you say it'll be no problem, why should I worry? Like Maggie, I have lots of confidence in you.' Then a stabbing pain, like a red-hot knife, jerked him upright. He fought to control his agonized expression, but Bradey, looking at him, felt a qualm.

'You're ill, aren't you, Mike?' he said. 'Look, we are working together. I like you. We have a big job to do. If there is a cock-up, we'll all land in the slammer. Each of us has a job to do. Maggie has to take care of the hotel dick. You have to put anyone unexpected out of action, I have to open the safe and get the Warrenton diamonds. We are a team. Level with me, Mike. You're ill, aren't you?'

Mike stared down at his big hands for a long moment, then he looked at Bradey.

'I'll be dead in six months,' he said. 'That's why I am doing this job. I have a terminal cancer.'

Bradey felt sweat turn his hands clammy.

Terminal cancer!

He had a horror of death. Here was this big, disciplined man telling him his big disciplined body would be in a box in six months' time, and yet, there was almost a serene expression in Mike's eyes.

'I don't give a damn about myself,' Mike said. 'I have had a good life. It's just one of those things, but I care a lot about my daughter. Don't worry. I need the money. I won't let you down.'

Bradey leaned forward, staring at Mike.

'Tonight, Mike. Suppose you get one of those pains when I need you most? Look, for God's sake, level with me. If you don't really think you can handle this job, we'll call it off. We can get out of here. I don't want to land in jail. I don't want Maggie to land in jail. For God's sake, Mike, level with me!'

Mike looked directly at him.

'I won't let you down,' he said, slowly and distinctly. 'I will do this job you hired me for. I have pain-killing pills. I hate pills, but tonight, I will use them. I give you my word, I'll do what you want me to do.'

Bradey, staring at this big man who was staring back at him, felt a surge of confidence.

'Okay, Mike,' he said. 'I don't have to tell you how sorry I am. I damn well am! Okay, coming from you, I know you'll do the job.'

At this moment, Maggie came in, wrapped in her towelling coat.

'I'm starving!' she exclaimed. 'When do we eat?'

'Maggie, baby,' Bradey said, 'you can make a complete hog of yourself. We'll be out of here tonight, and I won't have to foot the bill. We'll be off.'

Maggie squealed with excitement.

'You mean I can eat what I like?'

'That's what I mean,' Bradey said. 'You can work through the whole goddamn menu. Now, get us a drink.'

While Maggie made gin martinis which Mike refused, Bradey went through the plan of operation.

'As soon as Maggie has got this house dick in the shrubbery, we move in,' he said to Mike. 'I've all the equipment we need. This you can leave to me. First, we empty the security boxes, then we go down to the penthouse terrace. If the Warrentons aren't asleep, you will dart them. We collect the diamonds, then we walk out. There's nothing tricky about this. We go into operation as soon as Maggie handles the dick: around 02.45. At that time, there are few people around: most of them half drunk. We return here, wait for Maggie, take the Rolls and away we go. I'm seeing the boss after dinner. He'll set up a meeting-place. I'll have all that fixed by the time we begin the operation.'

Maggie sipped her drink.

'Oh, hon, I'll be sad to leave this lovely place. I've so enjoyed it.'

'There are other places,' Bradey said. He looked at his watch. 'I guess we can eat.'

Maggie clapped her hands.

'Let's go! I'm starving!'

'When ever aren't you?' Bradey said. 'How about you, Mike?'

Wrestling with another stabbing pain, Mike forced a grin.

'I guess I'll stay here. Have a ball!'

'You mean you are not going to *eat*?' Maggie cried, her eyes popping wide.

'Maggie!' Bradey snapped. 'Wheel me to the restaurant! Not everyone is such a hog as you!'

Startled, Maggie took hold of the wheel-chair and manoeuvred it out of the chalet.

'Imagine! With all this gorgeous free food, and he's not interested!' she said, as she rushed the wheel-chair towards the terrace restaurant.

'Slow down!' Bradey snapped. 'Do you think you're competing in the Grand Prix?'

Maggie reluctantly slowed down.

'I'm hungry, hon,' she whined.

'Don't repeat yourself!' Bradey said. He decided he wouldn't tell Maggie that Mike was a dying man. He knew Maggie was hopelessly sentimental. If she knew Mike would be dead in a few months time, she could collapse in snivelling tears and be utterly useless for the operation ahead.

As Maggie manoeuvred the wheel-chair onto the terrace restaurant, as the *maître d'* came swiftly to her side, Bradey relaxed.

You either win or lose, he thought as Maggie steered the wheel-chair to their corner table.

Eight million dollars!

This was the big take!

He had surveyed the penthouse. He knew he could open the safe and the boxes containing these too rich people's valuables. He was sure he would get the Warrenton diamonds. The deal looked good. He had confidence in Mike, in spite of his illness. He knew for certain Maggie would keep the hotel dick occupied.

Eight million dollars!

It was as good as being in his Swiss bank!

The thought made him hungry. Taking the menu from the *maître d'*, he glanced at the *Table d'hôte*: a five-course lunch.

'We'll take the lot,' he said, 'and a bottle of your best wine.'

Maggie gave a squeal of excitement that startled the old people already eating.

* * *

As the sun began to rise, Manuel Torres was busy with his boat. In the forward cabin, Fuentes lay sweating on the bunk, listening to Manuel's activities.

Fuentes was frightened to come out on deck, so he stifled in the little cabin, wondering if there was a cop patrolling the harbour, and cursing Manuel for ignoring him.

It wasn't until after midday that Manuel came down into the cabin.

'What the hell have you been doing?' Fuentes snarled. 'I've been lying here in this goddamn heat . . .'

'Yes, my friend,' Manuel said. 'I am sorry for you, but soon now, you will be home. Have patience.'

He went into the galley.

Wiping the sweat off his face, Fuentes went to the door of the galley.

'What is happening?' he demanded. 'How much longer do I have to stay in the cabin?'

Manuel put a pot of water on the stove. He threw in salt.

'My boat is ready to sail,' he said. 'We do the job tonight. We meet Anita at her place at midnight. We finalize the operation.' As the water began to boil, he fed in sticks of spaghetti. 'In a few days, we leave for Havana with five million dollars in my boat. We take Warrenton as hostage. No one will dare stop us.'

117

Fuentes sucked in his breath. He felt suddenly elated. How smart he had been to have gone to this man for help! Of course the boat! He had imagined they were going to hi-jack a plane! How much safer in a boat! With this rich man as hostage, there would be no problem. A perfect plan!

'You are a great man, Manuel!' he exclaimed. 'It is a splendid idea!'

Manuel began to cut up onions and tomatoes.

'Go away,' he said. 'I have much to think about. I think better alone.'

Fuentes, knowing he was incapable of thinking, withdrew to the cabin. In a few days, Manuel had said, they would be on their way to Havana with five million dollars. Manuel was a man of truth. When he said something, that something would happen. All the Cubans in this small colony had said so. They all said repeatedly, 'Manuel Torres is a man of truth. What he promises happens.'

Fuentes sat back on the bunk, his hands gripped between his knees. In a few days he would be worth a million dollars! The very thought of such a vast sum made his brain reel.

A million dollars!

What would he do with such a sum? Perhaps buy a farm? He shook his head. No, to work a sugar cane farm was too hard. Fuentes had left his home town because the daily cutting of sugar canes had been more than he could bear. Perhaps a boat? He could get a crew together and fish. He imagined himself, like Manuel, owning a big fishing vessel, but he wouldn't work as Manuel did who didn't even have a crew to help him.

He sat, thinking.

A million dollars!

No, he was thinking like a peasant, he told himself. Sugar canes! Fishing! Ridiculous! He would find a girl. With a million dollars, girls would be easy to find. He would buy a café-bar. The girl would run it and he would be the important *patron*, walking around, talking, meeting friends. Yes, this would be his future life!

Manuel came into the cabin and set down a big bowl of spaghetti.

'We eat,' he said.

It wasn't until the meal was over and Manuel was relaxed that he began to talk.

'I want you to know, my friend,' he said, staring directly at Fuentes, 'that this operation is not without its problems.'

Fuentes, who imagined that there could be no problems with Manuel in control, stiffened.

'Problems? What problems?' he asked nervously.

Manuel lit a cigarette and placed his big hands on the table. He looked beyond Fuentes at the dirty wall of the cabin as if Fuentes wasn't there, and he was talking aloud to himself.

'We will get into the penthouse because Anita has a duplicate pass-key.' He said. 'That is the first step. Then we capture these two rich people, tie up the woman and make the man telephone his father in Texas. His father will collect the five million dollars. This will take a little time. It has to be in cash: the bills no larger than a hundred dollars. This means, my friend, a lot of bills. He will be warned not to go to the police. With all his money, I am sure there will be no problem. I will explain to him that we will be leaving by boat and with his son, as hostage. When we arrive in Havana or some place, his son will be released. You take your share. I will then sail for some place with the rest of the money. All this seems to me acceptable. No police. No problems.' He paused and shifted his gaze down to Fuentes. 'Do you agree?'

Fuentes shifted uneasily.

'Yes, but you said just now there were problems.' He ran his hand over his sweating face. 'Now you are telling me there are no problems. I don't understand.'

'My friend, you easily forget,' Manuel said quietly. 'Our big problem is the wife of Pedro.'

Fuentes stared at him.

'Yes, but what is a woman? If she makes difficulties, I will slit her throat.'

Manuel shook his head.

'Then the cops will come into this. You are not thinking. There must be no killing. So far, with my plan, the cops won't come into it. The father will give us the money, and we go. No cops. If we kill Anita, what do we do with her body? We leave with this rich man, warning his wife to say nothing or else we kill him. No one will know what is happening. We get on the boat and sail away, but if we kill Anita, we are in the shit. Do you understand?'

Fuentes' sluggish mind tried to absorb what Manuel was saying, but he kept thinking of the million dollars he would soon be owning. He forced himself to think, then a cunning smile lit up his fat face.

'Is it such a problem?' he asked. 'We will all get on the boat, and when at sea, I will slit her throat. She will be for the sharks.'

Leaning forward, Manuel tapped his thick finger on the table as if spelling out each word.

'This is no ordinary woman. How do we get her on the boat without her husband who is dying and could be dead by now?'

Fuentes gave up. This was something his sluggish mind couldn't cope with.

'So what do we do?' he asked. 'You tell me I can't kill her. You tell me she won't leave the penthouse without this stupid husband of hers. What do we do?'

Manuel nodded.

'This is the problem. Unless I solve it, there will be no money for either of us.' He clenched his fists and slammed them down on the table. 'I have to solve this problem!'

Fuentes sat back. This was beyond him. He waited.

Manuel again appeared to be talking to himself, staring at the wall above Fuentes' head. 'I must lie to her: lie and lie and lie. I must have this money! My whole future will change with this money! I must lie to her! I must make her believe that she will have her husband. I must talk softly to her until I get her onto my boat. Yes, you are right, my friend, if, and only if, she becomes difficult, after she knows she is not getting her husband, then I will leave her to you.' He put his hands on his bald head and groaned. 'My people trust me. She trusts me. By doing this thing I am no longer a man of truth. For years now, I have lived as a man of truth.'

Listening, suddenly into Fuentes' small, cunning mind came a frightening thought.

If this man of truth could forsake the truth and betray one of his people, how safe was the million dollars this man of truth had promised to give him?

Suppose when they were on the boat with five million dollars, and Manuel had told him to slit Anita's throat? Would it stop there? Would this man of truth decide five millions were better than four? Would he suddenly club him and throw him after Anita to be eaten by the sharks?

He felt a shudder of fear run through him.

Manuel wasn't looking at him. He was now staring down at his big hands.

'This is the only solution. I must lie to her,' he muttered, 'and may God forgive me.'

Six

In a sour mood, Detective 1st Grade Tom Lepski sat at his desk in the detectives' room of the Paradise City Police headquarters. He was thumbing through the previous night's crime sheet reports, and muttering to himself.

His sour mood was caused by an argument he had had with his wife, Carroll: an argument he invariably lost and this soured him.

Lepski liked his bed. He had always a rush to get to police headquarters on time, but this didn't worry him. He had the rush timed to a second.

There was nothing he liked better than his breakfast: three eggs, grilled ham, toast, jam and coffee. At 07.15 Carroll rolled out of bed, went to the kitchen and prepared this meal while Lepski shaved, showered and threw on his clothes.

This morning, he had put on his shirt and was struggling into his trousers when his nose twitched. He couldn't smell the usual appetizing smell of grilling ham nor could he hear the sizzling of frying eggs. Puzzled, he zipped his trousers, then started towards the kitchen to find Carroll standing in the bedroom doorway, holding a juicy-looking ham steak at the end of the fork.

'Hi, honey,' Lepski said, pausing. 'How's my breakfast?'

'No clean shirt . . . no breakfast,' Carroll said in her bossy voice.

'Shirt?' Lepski gaped. 'What's a shirt to do with my breakfast?'

'You have not put on the clean shirt I put out for you last night.'

Lepski made a noise that would have startled a wild cat.

'Nothing's the matter with this goddamn shirt! Let's have breakfast.'

'That shirt is filthy!' Carroll said. 'Have you no pride?'

'Pride? What the hell has pride to do with my breakfast?'

'Lepski! You have worn that shirt for three days,' Carroll said, slowly and distinctly. 'It is a disgrace! I took the trouble to put out a clean one. Put it on!'

'One more day won't hurt. Let's have breakfast!'

'I will not have you, as a first Grade detective, looking like a bum! No clean shirt . . . no breakfast!'

Lepski hesitated. Time was running out. He wanted his breakfast, and seeing Carroll's determined stare, he moaned and tore off the offending shirt, scattering buttons. As he was putting on the clean shirt, Carroll gave a nod, then retired to the kitchen.

He was ten minutes late arriving at police headquarters. Max Jacoby was about to ride him, but seeing Lepski's sour expression decided to keep his mouth shut.

'Cubans!' Lepski suddenly exploded. 'Look at this mess last night!' He waved the crime reports in Jacoby's direction. 'Every goddamn night, these jerks start trouble! Refugees! Florida is getting as bad as Chicago!'

'Well, it keeps us employed,' Jacoby said.

The telephone on Lepski's desk came alive.

He snatched up the receiver and bawled, 'Lepski!'

'This is Larry. The fink who shot those two in the rent grab is coming to the surface. The quack says we can talk to him for three minutes. Do you want me to talk to him or you?'

'Me!' Lepski shouted. 'I'll be over there in ten minutes.' He slammed down the receiver. 'Come on, Max. This rent killer is coming to the surface. Let's go!'

On the way to the hospital with Lepski driving, Jacoby said, 'That's a pretty snappy shirt you're wearing, Tom.'

Lepski looked suspiciously at him, wondering if he was being conned.

'You think so?'

'Sure do. I don't know how you manage to wear so many clean shirts.'

Lepski looked smug.

'It's a matter of pride. After all, I'm the top cop around here. A top cop has to look well dressed. Talking about shirts, Max, that rag you're wearing is a disgrace.'

'I guess.' Jacoby sighed, 'but then I haven't a great girl like Carroll to look after me.'

Lepski scowled.

'What's she to do with it? Okay, she fixes the laundry, but anyone with pride should change his shirt every day. You'd better watch it.'

'Yeah.' Jacoby sighed. 'I'll watch it.'

Dr. Gerald Skinner, the head of the Paradise City Hospital, received them in his office. He was tall, thin, balding and busy.

'I understand you two officers want to interview this Cuban,' he said. 'I must make it plain that he is dying. There are favourable signs that he is recovering consciousness, but whether or not he will be coherent remains to be seen.'

'He's really going to croak?' Lepski asked, aware that he had shot down the young Cuban.

Skinner shrugged.

'I would have thought so, but he is young. We could just pull him through. The signs are not favourable. In intensive care, he might survive, and he's getting the best attention.'

Lepski snorted.

'He's killed two people. Who cares?'

Skinner looked coldly at him.

'We care,' he said. 'We have a reputation here for

saving lives, no matter what kind of life. I'll ask you to keep your interview with this man short.'

'Okay, Doc.'

Skinner pressed a bell push and a nurse came in.

'Take these two officers to room six,' he said. 'Good day to you,' and nodding, he picked up a bulky file.

Following the nurse, Lepski and Jacoby entered the room, set aside for Pedro Certes. By his bed, Larry Stevens, third-grade detective, sat in utter boredom. His round, freckled face lit up when he saw Lepski.

'The creep's making noises,' he said, getting to his feet. 'Okay for me to have breakfast?'

'Go ahead, Larry. Leave him to me.'

Lepski sat in the vacant chair by the bedside. Jacoby pulled up another chair and sat down, hopefully taking out his notebook and pencil.

Lepski regarded the man, lying in bed, and he grimaced. If ever there were signs of death, they were on the thin, white face of this Cuban.

They waited.

Five minutes crawled by, then Lepski began to lose patience. He took hold of Pedro's hot, thin wrist and gave it a sharp shake.

Pedro moaned, then opened his eyes.

'How are you feeling, son?' Lepski asked. His gentle voice startled Jacoby who had never heard Lepski in a kindly rôle.

Pedro groaned and closed his eyes.

'Listen, son, who are you?' Lepski asked, slowly and distinctly. 'What's your name?'

Pedro's eyes slowly opened.

'Go to hell,' he mumbled, and closed his eyes.

'Son, I have to tell you something. You are a very sick boy, and the doc tells me you're not going to make it. In a little while, you will be an unidentified corpse if you don't tell me your name,' Lepski said. 'Do you want that to happen?'

Pedro opened his eyes and stared at Lepski.

'An unidentified corpse,' Lepski repeated, a sad note in his voice that made Jacoby stare. 'Now, we don't like talking about this, but a lot of bums die in this city. We had an old rummy who died the other day. He had no papers. No one knew who he was. We tried to find his next of kin, but no one came forward. When the city gets landed with an unidentified corpse, know what happens? Funerals cost money. This old rummy was wrapped in a rubber sheet and was taken out to sea and fed to the sharks. You wouldn't want that to happen to you, would you, son?'

Listening, Jacoby gaped. He nearly spoilt Lepski's lies by protesting, but Lepski gave him his cop scowl and he controlled himself.

'No one wants to finish up as a shark's dinner, do they?' Lepski went on. 'If we know who you are, we can contact your family or your wife if you're married, and you'll be buried decently. You don't want to be chucked into the sea, do you?'

Pedro shivered, and a shadow of horror crossed his face. Knowing Cubans were not only religious but also superstitious, Lepski waited.

After a pause, Lepski went on, 'So, son, help us to give you a decent funeral.' He leaned forward. 'What's your name?'

Pedro's breathing became uneven.

'Sharks?' he mumbled.

'Yes, son, you know there are hungry sharks waiting out in the bay for a meal.'

Pedro shuddered.

'My name is Pedro Certes,' he finally whispered.

Still using his soft, kindly voice, Lepski asked, 'Where do you live, Pedro?'

'Twenty-seven, Fish Road, Seacomb,' Pedro muttered after a long hesitation.

'Have you a wife, Pedro? We'll go along and talk to her to give you a decent funeral.'

'Anita.'

'What does she do, Pedro? Where does she work?'

'She works. . . .' Pedro gave gasping sighs, closed his eyes and his face went slack.

'Get the nurse!' Lepski said sharply. 'Looks like he's going to croak.'

As Jacoby jumped to his feet, the nurse came in.

'Time's up,' she said briskly.

'He's in a state,' Lepski said.

The nurse came to the bed, took Pedro's pulse, then shrugged.

'He'll last a little longer,' she said, indifferently. 'Off you two go. I've things to do to him.'

Out in the passage, Jacoby said, 'That shark con was pretty rough, wasn't it?'

'It worked, didn't it? Now for Fish Road.'

Ten minutes later, the two detectives were talking to the Cuban janitor in charge of the shabby block of apartments where the Certes lived.

The janitor was a short, fat man with a black moustache and small cunning eyes.

'Pedro Certes? Sure, he lives here. Top floor, left.'

'Is his wife at home?'

'No. She works.'

'Where does she work?'

The janitor liked Anita. He had no time for Pedro, but Anita always passed the time of day with him. He wasn't giving out any information about Anita to a cop. His face went blank.

'I don't know.'

Lepski snorted.

'We want to find her fast. This is an emergency. Her husband is dying. We want to take her to him.'

The janitor sneered.

'One of our people is dying so two cops come for his wife. That's a big deal.'

'Do you or don't you know where she works?' Lepski barked.

'I told you. I don't.'

128

'What time does she get back from work?'

The janitor knew Anita's hours, but this he wasn't going to tell a cop. He shrugged.

'How do I know? Late, sometimes. I don't know.'

'What's she look like?'

So these two smart cops hadn't a description of Anita, the janitor thought. That was good news.

'Look like? Like any Cuban woman: dark, very fat, wears her hair on the top of her head.' That was as far as he could think of to mis-describe Anita.

'What age?'

'How do I know? Any age. Twenty, thirty, something like that.'

Lepski grunted, knowing he wasn't going to get any useful information from this Cuban. He jerked his head at Jacoby, then walked into the street.

'These goddamn Cubans all stick together,' he said. 'We'll have to stake out the place. You stick around, Max. I'll get two boys down here to relieve you. Check the papers of every Cuban woman, fat or thin, who goes into the building.'

'Nice job,' Jacoby said bitterly.

Lepski grunted, got in his car and headed fast for headquarters.

A few minutes later, the janitor came out onto the street, carrying a trash can which he dumped on the sidewalk. He spotted Jacoby, trying to interest himself in a display of fishing tackle in a shop window nearby.

The janitor returned to his apartment. He stood for a long moment in thought, then he called for his son: a dark-eyed, bright-looking boy of twelve years of age.

'You know Manuel Torres's boat,' his father asked him.

'Course I do! I know all the boats.'

'Right. Go there fast. Tell Mr. Torres that the cops have been here, asking for Mrs. Certes. Tell him they are watching our place. Understand?'

The boy nodded and leaving the building, passing Jacoby with a sly grin, he ran towards the waterfront.

* * *

Maria Warrenton had left her bathroom in such a mess,
Anita was late leaving the hotel. As she began the long
walk back to Seacomb, Manuel's battered Lincoln pulled
up beside her.

'Get in, Anita,' he said.

Anita opened the passenger's door and scrambled in.

'It's not Pedro? He's not worse?' she asked, her voice
trembling.

'No, he is okay.' Manuel shifted into gear and drove
down a side road that led to the waterfront. 'You mustn't
go home. The cops are asking for you.'

Anita gasped, covering her face with her hands.

'The cops?'

'Yes. Now don't get upset,' Manuel said. 'You must stay
on my boat until it is time for you to go to the hotel to
work. You must keep off the streets. I understand the
cops haven't a description of you. They questioned your
janitor and he told them nothing, but it will be safer for
you to stay on my boat a little while, then we can arrange
what we have to do tonight.'

'But how did they find my address?' Anita asked. 'Pedro
would never have given it to them.'

This Manuel didn't believe. He felt sure the cops had
talked to Pedro, and although he was dying, they had got
his name and address out of him.

'Pedro? No, certainly not! Some informer. Even with
our people, there are informers,' Manuel said. 'Don't
worry about it. All will be well.' He pulled up near his
fishing vessel. 'Now, we will make final plans.'

In the forward cabin, they found Fuentes lying on the
bunk. He sat up, staring at Anita.

'What's she doing here?' he demanded.

'It is unfortunate,' Manuel said quietly, sitting at the
table. 'The cops are looking for her. She will stay here
until she goes to work.'

Fuentes began to speak, but Manuel silenced him with a wave of his hand.

'Sit down, Anita.'

When she sat at the table, he went on, 'What time tonight should we begin the operation?'

'Twelve-thirty,' Anita said without hesitation. 'Everyone will be away from the suites. The hotel detective begins patrolling the corridors at one o'clock. The staff will be busy finishing in the kitchens. That is the time.'

'What time do you finish your work?'

'Just after ten o'clock. Give me a piece of paper and a pencil. I'll draw you a plan how to get to the staff entrance.'

Manuel produced paper and pencil and watched Anita draw the plan. While she was doing this, he glanced at Fuentes and gave him a nod to tell him Anita knew what she was about.

She passed him the paper.

'You see?'

Manuel studied the plan for some moments, then he nodded.

'So we come by the back, that is Ranch Road. We come down by the golf course, then down a little path leading to the staff entrance?'

'Yes.'

'Are there any problems?'

'No, but be careful not to be seen.'

'Then what happens?'

'At exactly twelve-thirty, I will open the staff door. You must be there to come in immediately. There will be no one about. I will take you to the basement elevator and we go up to the top floor. The penthouse suite where the Warrentons are has a private elevator. We walk up the stairs and I will unlock their door.'

'Suppose they are in?'

'They are never there until well after one-thirty. I will relock the door and we will go out onto the terrace and wait for them. The rest I leave to you.'

131

Manuel thought about this, aware that Fuentes was watching him.

Finally, he said, 'It sounds good.'

'Manuel,' Anita said quietly. 'It is understood that my husband comes with us.'

There was a long pause. Fuentes ran his fingers through his long, greasy hair. Manuel stared down at the scarred table, then he looked up and stared directly at Anita.

'Yes,' he said. 'That has always been understood. Pedro is recovering, but, Anita, by coming with us on my boat, he could have a relapse. He is still very sick.'

Anita stiffened.

'If you don't promise that he comes with us, I do not open the staff door,' she said firmly.

'I understand your feelings. You are a fine woman, but let us look more closely at the problem,' Manuel said, giving her a forced sympathetic smile. 'We have all we need to put on the pressure: two bombs and the Warrentons, but your husband is still very sick. In two weeks, he could travel without causing a relapse, but now the cops are looking for you, we can't wait two weeks. Our plan must begin tonight. I will now go to the hospital and talk to my friend and find out if Pedro can be moved. If he says he can, then there is no problem, but if he tells me it would be dangerous for Pedro to take a sea voyage, then I have another suggestion to make to you.'

Anita sat motionless, staring at Manuel. He felt uneasiness run through him. Her big black eyes were probing and hard.

'What other suggestion?' Her voice was low and harsh.

'That we need not discuss for the moment.' Manuel got to his feet. 'I will now go to the hospital and talk to my friend. I am hoping there will be no alternative. I will be back in an hour.'

'I will wait,' Anita said, 'but it is understood that unless Pedro comes with us, I open no doors.'

'It is understood,' and Manuel left the cabin, crossed the gang-plank, got in his car and drove away.

Fuentes stared at Anita, his eyes glistening with hate. He longed to pull out his knife and slit her throat. A million dollars, if he was lucky, was within his reach, but this woman could foul up the whole operation.

Anita didn't look at him. She stared down at her clenched fists.

'Manuel is a man of truth,' Fuentes said. 'You must do what he says. You must be reasonable.'

Anita looked up. The expression in her eyes made Fuentes slinch.

'You did this! It was you who persuaded my husband to do this dreadful thing! You gave him the gun! Don't speak to me! May God punish you!'

Fuentes had nothing to say. He lay back on the bunk and stared up at the roof of the cabin. This woman was dangerous, he thought. What lie would Manuel find to tell her?

* * *

When Lepski told Sergeant Joe Beigler that he now had the name of the rent killer and it was important to locate the killer's wife, Beigler, sipping coffee, said Lepski had done a smart job. However, when Lepski said he wanted two men down to Fish Road to stake out the apartment block and to relieve Jacoby, Beigler stared at Lepski as if he had asked for a ton of gold.

'I haven't two men to spare,' Beigler said, after a long pause.

'That's your headache. *I* want the joint staked out. I can't find out where this woman works, so the best thing is to catch her when she returns from work,' Lepski said patiently as if explaining to an idiot child.

Beigler drank more coffee.

'You know what I'd do if I were a smart first-grade detective?' he asked. 'I might add that I am not a smart first-grade detective, but a very smart sergeant. Now, if I wanted to know where some Cuban woman worked, know what I would do?'

Lepski loosened his tie. When Beigler became patronizing, Lepski's blood pressure rushed up.

'I'll buy it,' he snarled.

Beigler sat back, a smug smile on his freckled face.

'Being a very smart sergeant, and being in charge of this cop house while the chief is away, I would go down to the City Hall and inquire at the Aliens and Immigration office where they keep records of every Cuban working in our city and where they work.'

Lepski gaped at him.

'How the hell should I know that?'

'You wouldn't, but I do know these things being a very smart . . .'

But Lepski had already rushed away. He flung himself into his car and drove to the City Hall.

At the back of the City Hall, he found the Alien and Immigration office with a long queue of shabby-looking Cuban refugees waiting to register.

Lepski had no time for Cubans. He bulldozed his way into the big office where Cuban men and women were being interviewed.

Shoving his way to the head of the queue, he was confronted by a young woman, sitting behind a long counter, completing a card. The plaque before her told him she was Miss Hepplewaite.

He regarded her and decided she was a smarty pants, good-looking and efficient.

'Miss Hepplewaite?' He flashed his shield. 'Detective Lepski.'

She didn't look up, but continued to complete the card. Lepski wasn't to know that she had had an argument with a cop for a parking infringement that morning and had been given a ticket. Right at this moment, Miss Hepplewaite, a girl of exceptionally strong character, hated all cops.

Lepski waited, drumming his fingers on the counter.

When she had completed the card, she looked up, her grey-blue eyes stony.

'I am dealing with Cubans,' she said. 'Who did you say you were?'

Lepski loosened his tie.

'Detective Lepski, City police,' he said in his cop voice and again flashed his shield.

'What am I supposed to do?' she asked. 'Kneel down and worship you?'

A real smarty-pants, Lepski thought, controlling himself.

'Police business, Miss Hepplewaite. I want to find out where Anita Certes of twenty-seven, Fish Road, Seacomb, works.'

She regarded him with hostile eyes.

'Why?'

Lepski's blood pressure rose. He longed to haul her across the counter and smack her bottom.

'Police business,' he repeated. 'You don't have to worry your head about why, baby.'

'Don't call me baby! I could report you for being insulting!'

Lepski had had enough of this.

'Yeah, and I could arrest you for obstruction, baby. I'm dealing with a murder case. Do you want to come down to headquarters so we can sort it all out?'

Miss Hepplewaite regarded Lepski's lean, hard face and decided also enough was enough. He looked as if he would do what he was threatening. The last thing Miss Hepplewaite wanted was to be taken to police headquarters. She surrendered reluctantly.

'What name was it?'

Lepski gave her his hard, cop smile.

'Anita Certes, twenty-seven, Fish Road, Seacomb.'

'You understand we have many . . .' Miss Hepplewaite began, trying to bolster up her diminishing dignity.

'Anita Certes, twenty-seven, Fish Road, Seacomb,' Lepski barked.

'I'll see.' Furious with herself for being cowed by this cop, Miss Hepplewaite stamped over to the files. She deliberately took her time, while Lepski drummed on the counter and the Cubans stared and listened.

Finally, she returned with a card.

'This woman works part time at the Spanish Bay Hotel,' she said. 'Her hours are from ten o'clock to one o'clock and again at eight o'clock in the evening. She is a cleaner.'

Lepski gave her his leering smile.

'Thanks, baby. Keep your legs crossed,' and he left.

A small, thin Cuban, half way down the queue, whispered to his friend ahead of him. 'Hold my place,' and leaving, he went in search of a public telephone. He was a good friend of Anita Certes. There was only one man who could relay the news that Anita was being hunted by the police. He called Manuel Torres.

*   *   *

Josh Prescott, the Spanish Bay Hotel house detective, was preparing for his night's duty. He had showered, shaved and was now dressing. His mind had been continually thinking of this fantastic, glamorous nurse. He had been with dozens of girls, but none of them compared with her. They had a date this night. The thought of once more getting her into the shrubbery sent his blood pressure soaring. As he adjusted his tie, his front door bell rang.

Lepski barged in.

'Hi, Josh!'

'What do you want?' Prescott demanded. 'I'm getting ready to go on duty.'

'So what?' Lepski sat down. 'A Cuban woman who works at the hotel. Anita Certes. Mean anything to you?'

'Sure. She does the cleaning, part time. What about her?'

'You've read about this fink who shot to death the rent collector at Fish Road?'

136

Prescott nodded.

'Anita Certes is the killer's wife. I want to talk to her.'

'These goddamn Cubans are always in trouble.'

'You're right. I'm always saying that. This woman works from eight to ten. Right?'

'Yeah.'

'So I come to the hotel and talk to her, huh?'

Prescott thought for a moment, then shook his head.

'She services the Warrentons' penthouse, Tom. My boss would go out of his skull if the penthouse wasn't serviced. Look, to handle this right, wait until she comes off duty. I'll fix it to have her in my office just after ten. Then you can talk to her.'

Lepski, knowing Dulac's power in the city, shrugged.

'Okay, Josh. I'll be in your office just before ten.'

'I'll have her for you,' Prescott promised.

The time now was 18.30.

Lepski was hungry. Carroll had told him she was preparing a new dish, but had refused to tell him what it was. When Carroll wasn't spending hours on the telephone or going to coffee parties, yakking with her girl friends, she studied cook books. She was always finding some new complicated dish which invariably ended in disaster.

Lepski lived in the hope that one day, she would produce a meal that they could eat instead of falling back on cold cuts from the regrigerator.

As he opened his front door, the fumes of burning assailed him and the sound of Carroll's cursing singed his ears.

With what he hoped was a loving, understanding smile which, in fact, made him look like a man who had escaped from a horror movie, he walked into the smoke-filled kitchen.

* * *

Anita and Fuentes waited more than three hours before Manuel returned to his vessel. Those three hours were the worst hours Fuentes had ever experienced.

The cabin was stiflingly hot. He smoked continuously, moved restlessly, muttered to himself, and was always aware that this woman, sitting like a stone image, hated him.

From time to time, he glanced uneasily at her. She remained, staring down at her clenched fists, her thick, black hair, falling forward, half screening her face.

When he heard Manuel's thudding footfalls on the deck, he drew in a gasp of relief. Then, and only then, did Anita move. She lifted her head and stared at the cabin door, but her face was still like stone.

Manuel came in and shut the door. He went immediately to the table and sat down opposite Anita.

'Good news!' he said. Turning to where Fuentes was sitting up on the bunk, he went on, 'Get me a drink, my friend.'

Fuentes got a bottle of rum from a locker and poured a heavy shot into a glass.

'Anita, I regret being so long,' Manuel said. 'My friend at the hospital was busy. I had to wait.'

'Pedro?' Anita asked, huskily.

'Yes . . . Pedro.' Manuel took the glass from Fuentes and drank the raw rum, sighed and put the glass on the table. 'Finally, I talked to my friend. I explained the situation. I asked him if Pedro could take a sea trip. He said if things were properly arranged, Pedro could come with us. Pedro is now sitting up. He is taking food, but things will have to be properly arranged.'

Fuentes sat on the bunk, rubbing his sweating face, knowing that Manuel was lying, but he was lying convincingly.

'What things?' Anita demanded.

'My friend tells me Pedro must be taken from the hospital to my boat in an ambulance. Once on board, you

138

will be able to take care of him. There is no question of him being brought to the hotel. He must be spared the least exertion.'

Anita looked down at her clenched fists while she thought.

Fuentes felt sweat running down his face. This goddamn bitch of a woman! he thought. She stands between me and a million dollars!

Manuel also watched Anita, thinking she also held the key to five million dollars. Had he convinced her with his lies?

Anita looked up.

'Will the police let him come to the boat?' she asked.

'What else can they do? We have them by the short hairs,' Manuel said. 'It is fool proof. We will have Warrenton. We have two bombs. I will explain to Dulac that I can destroy his hotel from my boat if Pedro isn't put on board.'

She stared steadily at him.

'But can you do this?'

'Yes. The man who made the bombs owes me his life. He told me the bombs can be exploded by this device he has given me within a radius of two miles.'

Still, Anita continued to stare steadily at him.

'Show me this device.'

Manuel moved uneasily, but looking at her, seeing her hard stare, he got to his feet, went to a locker and took out a black box.

'This is the device,' he said. 'See: there are two buttons. I press the top one and the little bomb explodes. I press the bottom button and the big bomb explodes. I take this device with me.'

Anita stared at the black box which was the size of a packet of cigarettes.

'It will work?'

'Yes. It will work.'

She relaxed, and sitting back, she smiled at Manuel.

'Then Pedro and I will sail to Havana together sometime tonight?'

'Yes.'

She reached out her hand and put it on his.

'My good friend. It is truly said that you are a man of truth and a friend of my people. Thank you.'

The touch of her hand was like a searing hot iron, but Manuel managed not to flinch. Five million dollars! Who the hell wanted to be known as a man of truth when there was so much money to gain?

'So it is understood,' he said, moving his hands to scratch his beard. 'You open the doors, we kidnap the Warrentons, get the money, and you have Pedro.'

'It is understood,' Anita said, looking directly at him. 'I want a gun.'

'I have only two guns,' Manuel said, after a pause. 'One for me and the other for Fuentes. He and you will share the gun when you take it in turns to watch the Warrentons.'

Anita sat still. Under the cover of the table, her hand went to the handle of the knife, hidden by her black sweat shirt. She wouldn't need a gun if anything went wrong. A knife was silent. Her eyes shifted to Fuentes who was staring at her. This man she hated and distrusted.

'I know nothing about guns. Show me the gun I may have to use.'

Manuel went to a locker and took out a plastic sack. From it he produced a 3.8 revolver.

'There's nothing to it,' he said, handing the gun to Anita. 'It is not loaded. You hold the gun in both hands, aim and pull the trigger. It is important to hold the gun in both hands.'

Anita examined the gun thoughtfully while both men watched her, then she turned away, held the gun in both hands and pulled the trigger. The snap of the firing-pin made her start.

'Yes,' she said and handed the gun back to Manuel. 'I understand.'

Manuel put the gun back into the plastic sack and the sack into the locker.

'Let us eat,' he said. 'We may have to stay in the penthouse for two or three days. It is wise to eat.'

While he was preparing a meal of fish stew, Anita remained at the table, looking down at her hands.

Fuentes got off the bunk and went to the doorway of the galley. He had had enough of Anita's brooding expression.

Manuel winked at him, then pressed his thick fingers to his lips, signalling to Fuentes not to talk.

The meal was eaten in silence. As Anita was washing the dishes, the telephone bell rang. Manuel picked up the receiver, grunted 'Torres,' then listened. Finally, he said, 'Thank you. You have done well. I take care of my friends,' and he hung up.

Fuentes could see that Manuel was now worried. His heavy-featured face was set, and as he sat down at the table, he rubbed his bald, sweating head.

Anita came from the galley.

'Bad news,' Manuel said.

Anita stiffened, losing colour.

'Pedro?'

'No. Don't I keep telling you Pedro is all right?' Manuel snapped. 'Don't keep thinking of him!'

'I have nothing else to think about except my husband. What is the bad news?'

'The cops have found out you are working at the hotel.'

Anita flinched, then sat down at the table.

'What will happen?'

'I don't know. Maybe the police will be waiting for you. They will question you. They will talk to your boss: it is a dangerous situation.'

Anita thought while Manuel and Fuentes watched her: both men fearing that, after all, this great sum of money wouldn't materialize.

Anita looked up. Manuel marvelled at her calm expression.

141

'It will be all right,' she said. 'The hotel is short of staff. I am the only one who knows how to service the penthouse. For tonight, the hotel can't do without me. The questioning will come after I have done my work. I am sure, and then it will be too late.' She got to her feet. 'I will go now. I am not afraid of the police. At exactly twelve-thirty tonight, I will open the staff door. I give you my word.'

Manuel stared at her and relaxed.

'You are a fine, courageous woman,' he said. 'We will be there at exactly twelve-thirty.'

'It is understood in a day or so, we will sail for Havana with Pedro?'

'It is understood,' Manuel said with a false smile.

Anita looked directly at him.

'I trust you,' she said. 'You take all the money. I only want Pedro.'

When she had gone, there was a long, uneasy silence, then Fuentes said, 'This woman frightens me. She is dangerous. She mustn't be given a gun.'

Manuel shook his head.

'There is no question of that.' He pulled from his hip pocket what looked like a black sausage. This object he laid on the table. 'I have thought deeply about this since I left you. Pedro is dying. There is no other solution. I regret it, but we must keep the cops out of this affair. Anita will expect me to threaten the hotel owner to persuade the mayor to release her husband. She will stand by me while I talk to Dulac. If I do this, Dulac will alert the police. This is something we must avoid. I am sure, without Pedro, we will get the money. That I am truly sure of, but Anita must be neutralized.' He picked up the sausage-shaped object. 'A little tap on her head with this and she will no longer be a problem. She won't be damaged. I know well how to strike with a sand-bag.' He took from his pocket a roll of adhesive tape. 'As soon as she gets us into the penthouse, I will give her a little tap. We bind and gag her and take her out onto the terrace. Regretfully, there is no other way. When we get the money, we will release her. If she accepts the fact that Pedro is as good as dead and can't come with us but she agrees to come with us, then I will give her some money. If she is stupid, then regretfully, I will give her another tap and we leave her. By then, we will have the money and Warrenton as hostage. What can she do or the cops do? There is no other solution.'

Sweat began to run down Fuentes' face. He stared with alarm at the black sand-bag Manuel was holding.

He thought of the time when he, Manuel and Warrenton, as hostage, would be on the boat, heading for Havana.

I know well how to strike with a sand-bag.

Was that going to happen to him, then the sharks?

Manuel was regarding him.

'What is in your mind, my friend?' he asked.

My friend? This man of non-truth calling me friend, Fuentes thought.

'I am thinking of the money,' he said, forcing a smile. 'I was thinking what it would mean to me to own a million dollars.'

'Yes,' Manuel said quietly, 'but first we must get the money. Isn't that right, my friend?'

Into Fuentes' sluggish mind came a thought. He would have a gun. He would never take his eyes off Manuel during the voyage to Havana. When they were approaching the harbour lights, he would shoot Manuel. He had enough experience with boats to bring the boat into the harbour. There would be five million dollars on board! He would then shoot Warrenton, dock the boat and disappear with this enormous ransom!

This would have to be thought about, but there was time.

Five million dollars!

His face lit up as he said, 'Yes, you are right. First, we must get the money.'

* * *

Ed Haddon was sitting at the corner table at the
sea-food restaurant as Bradey joined him.

The *maître d'* hovered.

'Have the curried prawns,' Haddon said. 'They're
good.'

Bradey said curried prawns were fine with him. Haddon ordered another dry martini for himself and a Scotch
on the rocks for Bradey.

As soon as the *maître d'* had left them, Haddon looked
inquiringly at Bradey.

'What's the news?'

'We do the job tonight,' Bradey said. 'It looks a cert.
First, the safe, then the Warrentons' diamonds. So then
what happens?'

'You have your end completely tied up?'

'I told you: it's a cert.'

'I have my end tied up too,' Haddon said. 'Lu, we're
heading fast for the big deal.'

Two waiters arrived and served the curried prawns.
Haddon could see by Bradey's expression as he surveyed
his plate, that further business talk would be so much
waste of time.

The two men ate in silence. Every now and then,
Bradey made a loud humming noise of appreciation.
Finally, finished, he sat back, mopped his mouth with his
napkin and smiled.

'That, Ed, was devilish good.'

'Can you not turn your greedy mind to business?'
Haddon asked.

'Let's have the apple pie,' Bradey said. 'I'm a sucker for
apple pie.'

Haddon shrugged. He ordered two apple pies. While
they waited, Bradey picked his teeth and hummed under
his breath. Haddon contained his impatience with an
effort.

It wasn't until coffee and brandy had been served that Bradey became receptive.

'As I told you, I have my end tied up,' Haddon said. 'I've talked to Kendrick. He'll handle the whole deal. Now I know you'll do the job tonight, I'll alert him to have his fag at your chalet at two o'clock. You get the stuff and return to your chalet. Kendrick's fag will take the loot, and that's the end of your problem. Kendrick tells me he will stash the stuff away where no one will find it. When the heat dies down, he will sell the stuff. It may take a couple of months before we get the money, but no longer.'

Bradey grimaced.

'Suppose Kendrick says he's never had the loot? I don't trust that fat fag.'

Haddon smiled grimly.

'No problem, Lu. I have enough on Kendrick to put him out of business and into jail. We'll get the money.'

Bradey nodded.

'Okay. If you say so, Ed, then we get the money.'

'As soon as you've handed over the loot, you get back to your wheel-chair. You stay at the hotel for another two days. There'll be a check, but the cops won't even suspect you. Your papers are foolproof. After two days, you leave. Okay?'

'Yeah. I see that. How about my money, Ed?'

'Kendrick will pay your share into your Swiss bank in a couple of months time.'

'How about Bannion's money—fifty thousand?'

'He'll also have to wait.'

'Look, Ed,' Bradey said earnestly. 'This guy really needs the money. He's got a terminal cancer and an idiot child to take care of. To get a real performance from him, I want to promise him he gets his cut as soon as the job is done. Will you advance the money?'

'What's all this about? Who cares? If you feel like this, Lu, you advance him the money,' Haddon growled.

'I would if I had it, but I never seem to have any

money,' Bradey said. 'Now, come on, Ed. What's fifty thousand to you? Don't let us foul up this sweet job for the sake of fifty thousand, I want to promise Bannion that he gets paid off the moment the job has been done, and I want to keep that promise.'

'At my expense?'

'You're getting eight million, probably more, for the love of mike, Ed, be human!'

Haddon brooded, then shrugged.

'Oh for God's sake!' He grinned at Bradey. 'You could sell an egg to a hen. Okay, if Bannion does a good job, if you get the Warrenton diamonds, if you get the loot from the boxes, I'll give you fifty thousand for Bannion.'

Bradey smiled.

'It's a deal, Ed.' He pushed back his chair and stood up. 'Bannion will do a good job, and so will I. Thanks for a great meal. See you,' and he left the restaurant, got in his car and drove back to the Spanish Bay Hotel.

Seven

Maria and Wilbur Warrenton returned to the penthouse suite soon after 19.00. They had spent the afternoon surf-sailing and Wilbur was pleasantly relaxed. He looked forward to a quiet dinner at the hotel's restaurant, then to spend the rest of the evening watching a Spaghetti western on TV. His hopes were dashed, when Maria said, 'Please get my diamonds. I am in the mood to gamble. I feel I have a winning streak. We will dine at the Casino, then we will play.'

So much for the Spaghetti western, Wilbur thought as he said, 'But, Maria, I thought we had agreed you shouldn't wear your diamonds away from the hotel.'

Frowning, Maria lifted her eyebrows.

'When I want to wear my diamonds, I will wear them! Why have them if I don't wear them?'

'This city is full of starving, refugee Cubans,' Wilbur said patiently. 'Your diamonds could be a big temptation. There could be a hold-up.'

'Don't be so ridiculous! I am wearing my diamonds! We will leave at eight-thirty. You had better change,' and Maria went into her bedroom, slamming the door.

Wilbur thought for a long moment, then he went to the safe, twirled the combination, opened the safe door and took from it a leather jewel case. This he put on an occasional table, after relocking the safe. Then going to the telephone, he called Jean Dulac's office.

147

'This is Mr. Warrenton,' he said when a woman answered. 'I would like to speak to Mr. Dulac.'

'Certainly, Mr. Warrenton.' The bow in her voice pleased him. A moment later, Dulac came on the line. 'Good evening, Mr. Warrenton. Is there something I may do for you?'

'We are going to the Casino,' Wilburn said. 'Mrs. Warrenton will be wearing her diamonds.'

Dulac who had an uncanny talent for anticipating the wishes of his rich clients, said, 'I understand, Mr. Warrenton. You would like to have an efficient bodyguard to accompany you. That presents no problem. What time will you be leaving?'

'Around eight-thirty,' Wilbur said, startled that Dulac should immediately understand the situation.

'Then I will have a reliable bodyguard waiting in the lobby at eight-thirty. I will telephone Mr. Hendrick who runs the Casino. A bodyguard will be with you during your stay at the Casino and will accompany you back here. Is that satisfactory?'

'I'll say it is, and many thanks. Mr. Dulac, you run a great hotel,' Wilbur said, and meant it.

'It is my pleasure to serve you, Mr. Warrenton,' Dulac said smoothly. 'Have a nice night,' and he hung up.

Josh Prescott had just finished a dinner of steak and fried onions in the staff restaurant when a bell boy rushed up to him, telling him the Boss wanted him pronto.

Cursing under his breath, Prescott hurried to Dulac's office. The time now was 19.30.

'You are to act as bodyguard to Mr. and Mrs. Warrenton,' Dulac told him. 'They are going to the Casino, and Mrs. Warrenton will be wearing her diamonds. I have arranged with the Casino management to have a man take over from you. When you have safely conveyed Mr. and Mrs. Warrenton to the casino, you will return here and resume your duties.'

'Yes, sir,' Prescott said woodenly, thinking: These bloody rich bitches, showing off their goddamn diamonds!

'They will be leaving at eight-thirty,' Dulac went on. 'Wait for them in the lobby. Be there at eight o'clock. They must not be kept waiting.'

Prescott remembered he was planning to talk to Anita Certes when she arrived for work. By having to sit in the lobby at 20.00, he would miss her.

'Sir,' he said. 'You should know we have a part-time cleaner working on Mr. Warrenton's suite. She is a Cuban, and her husband is being held by the police for murder.'

Dulac flinched. One of his staff the wife of a murderer!

'We can't have a woman like that working here,' he said. 'What is her name?'

'Anita Certes, sir.'

'Very well, Prescott. Leave this to me.'

When Prescott left the office, Dulac telephoned his staff manager who moaned when Dulac told him to dismiss Anita Certes immediately.

'Not tonight, sir,' he pleaded. 'I have no extra staff to replace her. She does a good job. May I suggest I see her in the morning when I will be able to replace her?'

'Very well,' Dulac said, 'but we must get rid of her.'

While this conversation was taking place, and while Prescott was checking his revolver in his office before settling in the lobby to await the Warrentons, Anita arrived. She was early, hoping that the police weren't already at the hotel. No one saw her as she unlocked the staff door, closed and relocked it. She walked silently and swiftly to the women's rest room and locked herself in a toilet.

Sitting on the lid of the toilet seat, she prepared herself for a long wait. She had no intention of going up to the penthouse suite. It was just possible a cop or Prescott would be waiting up there. She would wait until 24.30 when she would unlock the staff door and then take Manuel and Fuentes up to the penthouse. Thinking about this, she decided the cops would wait in Prescott's office until she had finished her work. She was well aware that

149

the Spanish Bay Hotel would not tolerate cops roaming around to scare the rich and the spoilt.

Sitting in the semi-darkness, she thought of her beloved Pedro. How good it would be when they were on the boat together, heading back to his home! She longed to put her arms around him and comfort him. She felt sure once he was with her, she could nurse him back to health. She would slave in the sugar cane fields, earning money. He could lie in bed at his father's house until he was well enough to work by her side.

She slid off the toilet seat and onto her knees. She began to pray that in a few days Pedro and she would be united.

While she prayed, Pedro Certes moved from pain-ridden life into peaceful death.

* * *

Bradey, Maggie and Bannion sat in the chalet checking on last-minute details for the night's operation.

Bradey had told Bannion he had talked to the big Boss.

'We get the loot, Mike,' he said, 'and you get fifty thousand dollars. You may have a couple of days to wait, but no longer.'

Bannion hunched his massive shoulders.

'That's great news,' he said.

Maggie patted his hand.

'I love it for you, Mike.' She spoke from her sentimental heart. 'I do hope all will go well for your little daughter. I really mean it.'

Bannion had taken three pain-killing pills. Although he now felt no pain, he was worried. He wasn't moving as easily as usual. He found his feet dragged, and there was no spring in him. He suspected he was now dying faster than he thought he would die.

'You have a tuxedo with you, Mike?' Bradey asked.

'I have it.'

'I'll fix your face so no one will know you,' Bradey went

on. 'We both go to the hotel around two o'clock. No one will pay any attention to us. If anyone gets in our way, you will fix them with the dart. Remember the shot must be in the flesh: hand, face or neck. The Warrentons could be in the penthouse by the time we get there. You will dart them. The job shouldn't take more than forty minutes. We return here, hand the loot over to the Boss's man, and then we stay put for two more days. You get your money, and we say goodbye. Okay with you?'

Bannion nodded.

'You can rely on me.'

'I know I can. I know what this job means to you.' Bradey turned to Maggie. 'Now, honey, I don't have to tell you again what you have to do. You keep the hotel dick out of our hair. Now, another thing, and this will make your day. Go to the restaurant and tell the *Maître d'* I am unwell and won't be eating.'

Maggie's eyes widened in alarm.

'Oh, hon! Are you unwell?'

'You are to tell him that!' Bradey snapped. 'I'm fine! When the cops start checking, I want them to know I was in bed, unwell. Get it?'

Maggie gaped for a long moment, then smiled.

'That's smart. For a dreadful moment, I thought . . .'

'Never mind. You shouldn't think, Maggie. It doesn't do your brain any good. When you go to the restaurant check to see if the Warrentons are eating. See if you can find out if they are off some place for the night.'

'Yes, hon.' Maggie looked anxiously at Bradey. 'Can I eat at the restaurant?'

'You can stuff yourself blind,' Bradey said. 'Have the lot.'

Maggie gave a squeal of delight.

While they were talking, Bannion was thinking of his daughter, Chrissy. He had telephoned the Home twice since he had been in Paradise City. The nurse in charge had been kind and reassuring. Chrissy, she told him, was happy, but she missed him, and kept asking when she

151

would see him. Bannion, remembering those weekends when he was always with Chrissy, felt a pull at his heart. He told the nurse it wouldn't be long. She promised to tell Chrissy.

Half an hour later, Maggie, wearing her best party dress and looking like an escapee from *The Crazy Horse* revue, Paris, walked into the hotel lobby.

She saw Josh Prescott sitting glumly in a chair away from the chattering mob. She moved by him, rolled her hips and gave him her sexiest smile, then she entered the restaurant.

The *maître d'* advanced towards her while the elderly men, already eating, paused and regarded her, wishing they were twenty years younger.

'Good evening, madam,' the *maître d'* said. 'Mr. Vance is not with you?'

'The poor old dear is not well,' Maggie said, her big eyes sorrowful. 'He has these turns. He insisted I had dinner. He is so kind.'

'Can I send him a tray, madam?' The *maître d'* asked, escorting Maggie to the corner table.

Maggie paused. She saw the Warrentons walk into the lobby. She saw Prescott get hastily to his feet and join them. She saw the diamonds. Then the Warrentons and Prescott moved out of sight.

'Can I send a tray to Mr. Vance? Something very light?' the *maître d'* asked again.

'No, thank you. Mr. Vance is sleeping. I have given him a sedative.' She sat down at the table. 'Wasn't that Mr. and Mrs. Warrenton just leaving?'

'Yes, Madam. They are spending the evening at the Casino,' the *maître d'* replied and unfolded the spacious menu. 'Perhaps I can make some suggestions.' He thought this nurse was the most glamorous, sexy woman ever to come to the hotel.

Maggie suppressed a squeal of excitement. She gave him her wide-eyed, helpless look.

'Would you?' she said. 'I'm hungry.'

* * *

At the Casino restaurant, Maria Warrenton made a sensational entrance, as accompanied by Wilbur, the *maître d'* leading the way, she walked down the red-carpeted aisle, bordered by tables to the best table in the room.

The rich were already eating. Dinner was served early at the Casino. The main interest was the roulette tables. There was always a rush to get the meal over, and get to the business of the evening.

This was the first time many of the rich had seen the fabulous Warrenton diamonds. The men eyed Maria first, then the diamonds and envied Wilbur. The women had only eyes for the glittering collar, the ear-rings and the bracelets.

Maria was at her most difficult when choosing her dinner. There were times when Wilbur, who was always happy with a good steak, found it difficult to restrain his impatience as Maria insisted always to have every item on the menu explained to her by servile *maître d's*. Now, aware every woman in the room was watching her, she behaved with the petulant arrogance of a spoilt movie star.

Wilbur thought, 'Oh well, it's her honeymoon! Let her enjoy herself. I hope to God she doesn't act this way when we get home!'

Josh Prescott, having spoken to the Casino's detective and had his assurance that he would remain close to the Warrentons and would convey them back to the hotel, decided his duty was done.

He took a taxi back to the hotel and turned his thoughts to Maggie. He checked his watch. The time was now 21.00. He had this date with Maggie at 02.15. He had more than five hours to wait! Maggie had really turned him on. His mind was so preoccupied with her that he forgot about Anita Certes. Even when he began his patrol of the hotel corridors, he still forgot about her. His eyes continually checked the slow movement of the hour hand of his watch. He could only think of the moment when he and Maggie would be lying on the soft lawn, hidden by flowering shrubs.

* * *

From the plastic sack, Manuel produced two 3.8 revolvers which he laid on the table.

'Time moves,' he said. 'We mustn't be late. Be careful with this gun,' and he pushed one of the revolvers over to Fuentes. 'It is loaded. Remember, there is to be no shooting. This job can be handled without police interference.' He stared steadily at Fuentes. 'You understand? We only shoot if things go badly wrong.'

Fuentes licked his dry lips as he took the gun.

'I understand.'

'It may take three or four days before old man Warrenton comes up with the ransom,' Manuel went on. 'I will have to talk to Dulac. All of us will need food while we wait. He won't want his kitchens destroyed, so he will co-operate. You and I will take it in turns to sleep. The Warrentons will have to be bound. Anita will also have to be bound and gagged. It won't be easy, my friend, but to earn five million dollars can never be easy.'

'One million for me, and four for you,' Fuentes said quickly.

'Yes. That is correct.' Manuel smiled, but watching closely, Fuentes saw the smile didn't reach the black, stone-like eyes.

'If we have to stay in the penthouse for three or four days, these people will have to be fed. They will have to relieve themselves,' Fuentes said.

'Food will be provided by the hotel. There will be toilets in the penthouse.'

'When Anita recovers from the tap,' Fuentes said, 'she will be dangerous. Is it wise to release her hands?'

'That is something we will deal with when we are all together in the penthouse,' Manuel said. 'Don't worry about trifles. You must leave all the details to me, my friend.'

Fuentes shrugged.

'I am nervous about her. She is dangerous.'

Manuel smiled again: an evil smile.

'I am even more dangerous, my friend.'

The two men stared at each other. Fuentes felt a cold chill of fear run down his sweating back.

The sound of the telephone bell made both men start.

Manuel got up, crossed to the telephone and picked up the receiver.

'Torres,' he said, then listened while Fuentes fingered the gun, thinking, with this gun, he could handle Manuel. The feel of the cold butt gave him confidence.

Manuel said, 'Thank you, my friend. In a little while you will be rewarded,' and he hung up. He turned and smiled at Fuentes. 'If one has patience, most problems solve themselves,' he said. 'We now have no problem with Anita. My friend at the hospital tells me Pedro died half an hour ago.'

Fuentes stiffened.

'He's dead?' His face lit up. 'Good news!' He thought while Manuel watched him. 'When she knows, she might not let us into the penthouse.'

'She won't know. She is already at the hotel, waiting for us. When we get into the penthouse, I will tell her Pedro had a relapse and has died. There is nothing she can do about it. We will be in the penthouse. The cops are looking for her. She will have to come with us. I will even give her some money.'

'She may think you are lying,' Fuentes said uneasily. 'Suppose she thinks Pedro hasn't died. She could be dangerous.'

Manuel went to a locker and took from it a tiny radio transistor which he put in his pocket.

'I don't even have to tell her myself. It will be on the

155

news. You and I will be as surprised as she will be.' He put the revolver and a handful of cartridges in his other pocket. 'If she becomes hysterical, I will give her a little tap. Luck is going our way, my friend. Now we will go to the hotel.'

Manuel went first, then Fuentes followed him. They crossed the crowded quay to Manuel's car.

As Manuel started the car's engine, he patted Fuentes on his arm.

'All is going well,' he said. 'Soon, my friend, we will be rich.'

As Manuel drove off the quay, Fuentes fingered his gun.

* * *

At 21.45, Lepski, with Max Jacoby at his side, drove to the side entrance of the Spanish Bay Hotel. Both men were in a sour mood. Carroll had expected to be taken out that evening. Lepski, who never remembered anniversaries, even his wedding anniversary, had forgotten this day was the anniversary of their first trip to Europe. Although the trip had been a disaster, Carroll had said firmly she wanted to be taken to some decent restaurant and remember the few good times they had had. Lepski who scarcely ever listened to Carroll's chatter had muttered this was fine, and had immediately forgotten the arrangement. He had rushed into his home, expecting his dinner, and was astonished to find Carroll in the bath.

'Hey, baby!' he bawled. 'What's for dinner?'

'We are eating out, Lepski,' Carroll said coldly, glaring at him. 'We have a date.'

Lepski closed his eyes. He now remembered something about a celebration.

'Look, honey,' he said in his most wheedling voice. 'I've got police business. I'll be out for a couple of hours. I've got to interview the wife of this rent killer. How about some dinner?'

He received a soapy sponge right in his face.

He and Jacoby ate a burger snack while Lepski listened to Jacoby moan that he had had to stand up a blonde who appeared willing for action. Neither men talked as Lepski drove to the Spanish Bay Hotel. Parking the car, Lepski led the way to Josh Prescott's office which they found in darkness. Turning on the light, they took chairs, lit cigarettes and waited.

They sat in sullen silence. Anxiously, Lepski tried to think how he could placate Carroll when he returned home. When Carroll was frustrated, she could be more than difficult. Maybe, after he had talked to this goddamn Cuban, he would buy a big bouquet of flowers from the flower shop in the hotel which remained open long after midnight. Getting a bouquet of choice flowers from the Spanish Bay Hotel surely would sweeten Carroll. Then he thought what the bouquet would cost, and he flinched. Well, maybe not a bouquet. He'd buy a single rose, nicely packed in a gift box. Jacoby was thinking gloomily that his blonde date had many men friends. He might lose her for good.

Brooding so deeply on their troubles, the two detectives lost count of time. Suddenly, Lepski who had run out of cigarettes, glanced at his watch. The time now was 22.30. He started to his feet.

'What's going on?' he exclaimed. 'Josh said he would have the woman here at ten o'clock. It's now half past.'

'Maybe he's held up, or something,' Jacoby offered. 'If you want a cigarette have one of mine.'

'I'm going to look for him,' Lepski said. 'You stay here in case he shows up.'

He made his way to the night porter's desk. There were a number of men and women in evening dress in the lobby, about to enter the restaurant. Lepski, feeling self-conscious, slid around them and arrived at the night porter's desk.

'Seen Prescott?' he asked, flashing his shield.

The night porter, thin and elderly, regarded him as if he were a big, hairy spider.

'No doubt, Mr. Prescott is on patrol,' he said stiffly.

'Yeah, but where? I want to talk to him: police business,' Lepski said.

'Patrolling,' the night porter said. 'He could be anywhere.'

Lepski loosened his tie.

'Well, if you see him, tell him Detective Lepski is in his office.'

'*If* I see him,' the night porter returned who had no time for hotel dicks nor cops. 'He could be anywhere.'

Fuming, Lepski stamped back to Prescott's office. Jacoby was lighting yet another cigarette.

'The fink's on patrol,' Lepski snarled. 'I'll have one of those!'

It wasn't until after 23.15 that Prescott, his mind still on Maggie, his eyes continually on the hour hand of his watch, decided to look in at his office for a snort of Scotch and a new packet of cigarettes.

He came to an abrupt stop when he saw Lepski and Jacoby glaring at him. Then with a sense of shock, he remembered Anita Certes. He wasn't a tough ex-cop for nothing. Hitching on a wide smile, he entered the office.

'Hi, boys,' he said. 'Sorry about this. A foul-up. I had a special job escorting the Warrentons to the Casino. One of those things.'

'Where's the Cuban woman?' Lepski snarled.

'I guess she's home by now.'

Lepski got to his feet. He released a noise a clap of thunder might have envied.

'Home? What do you mean? You promised to have her here at ten o'clock. We've been sitting on our asses for goddamn hours, waiting!'

'I told you it was a foul-up. I had this job to do. She's home by now.'

'How do you know?' Lepski bawled.

'She comes here at eight. She leaves at ten. It is now

eleven-thirty,' Prescott said. 'And listen, Lepski, you
don't bawl at me. You may be the hot shot away from this
hotel, but I'm the hot shot here. If you want to talk to her,
go to her home.'

'How do I know she's at home?' Lepski demanded.

'Go and find out!' Prescott snapped. 'Where else should
she be?'

'She could have dropped dead in the penthouse.'

'So could Mickey Mouse. I tell you she's gone home!'

Jacoby got to his feet.

'Come on, Tom, let's go and see.'

Lepski snorted.

'If she isn't there, Prescott, I'll be back, and I'll start
something that'll put years on your life!'

'You start something in this hotel,' Prescott said, glaring
at Lepski, 'and I'll fix it Mr. Dulac, the mayor and your
chief get you back in uniform. Now, piss off!'

While this fracas was going on, Anita Certes who had
been continually looking at her watch, moved restlessly
on the lid of the toilet seat. Would it never get to
twelve-thirty? She began to pray again. She prayed,
waited and prayed again. She could hear the noise from
the kitchens gradually dying down. She heard the night
staff begin to leave. Finally, at a minute before twelve-
thirty, she moved out of the women's rest room. She
looked up and down the corridor, listened, then at exactly
24.30, she ran swiftly to the staff door, unlocked it and
opened it. She found Manuel and Fuentes waiting. She
beckoned them in, then led them to the elevator. The
three of them entered as the door swished open. Anita
pressed the top floor button. As the elevator ascended,
she looked at Manuel.

'Pedro?'

'No news,' Manuel lied. 'I tried to get my friend at the
hospital, but he had gone home. Don't worry. All will be
well.'

'I have been praying,' Anita said, looking trustingly at
Manuel. 'I feel in my heart all will be well.

159

'Yes,' Manuel said, hating himself. 'Your prayers will be answered.'

Reaching the top floor, Anita first checked the empty corridor, then led the two men up a flight of stairs to the door leading to the penthouse suite. It took her only a moment to unlock the door with her duplicate pass-key. The three of them entered the spacious living-room, dimly lit by the lamps from the terrace.

Anita closed and locked the door.

* * *

It was while Lepski was driving furiously to Seacomb that the news of Pedro Certes' death came over the car radio.

'So the creep's dead,' Jacoby said. 'Look, Tom, do we need to talk to his wife? What's the point?'

'You've got your blonde date still on your mind?' Lepski asked, easing his speed.

'Well, I might just catch her. She keeps late hours, and it's my day off tomorrow. I can sleep late. What do you expect from this Cuban? What's your thinking?'

'She might give us a line on Fuentes.'

'So what? He's in Havana. We can't get at him. For the love of Mike, let's go home. It's getting on for midnight. Who cares about a goddamn Cuban woman?' Jacoby said. 'The killer's dead. That closes the case. We have plenty of other work to do without bothering about a small-time killer who is now dead.'

Lepski pulled to the kerb.

'Yeah. I guess you're right. Okay, let's go home. I'll drop you off. Good luck, Max. I hope you make your date.'

'That makes two of us,' Jacoby said.

When Lepski left Jacoby at his apartment block, he headed for home. It wasn't until he had garaged his car that he remembered he had forgotten to buy Carroll a rose.

Feeling like a man going to his execution, he entered his home, locked the front door, then removing his shoes, stole to the bedroom, hoping Carroll would be asleep.

But, of course, she wasn't. She was sitting up in bed, waiting for him.

* * *

Anita said, a little breathlessly, 'Don't put on the lights.'

'No. We can see well enough from the lights on the terrace,' Manuel said, as he looked around. 'How the rich live!' The thought flashed through his mind that he too could have a penthouse like this when he had five million dollars. 'Well, we must sit and wait.' He sat down in one of the big lounging chairs as Fuentes, uneasy, went out onto the terrace. He was astonished at the size of the terrace, the large pots of flowers, the lounging chairs, tables and the cocktail bar.

'What is the time?' Manuel said, then peered at his watch in the semi-darkness. 'Ah! It is nearing news time. I have put money on a horse, Anita. I feel this is my lucky day.' He took from his pocket the tiny transistor. 'Do you ever back the horses?'

'I have no money for such things,' Anita said curtly. 'You are not going to turn that on? Someone might hear it.'

'No one will hear it,' Manuel said. 'I have to know if my horse has won,' and he switched on the transistor, adjusting the control so the sound was low but distinct.

Fuentes came to the doorway, his back to the moonlit terrace. Sweat was running down his face. Would this stupid woman begin to scream when she learned her creep of a husband had died? Would Manuel be able to control her? Once again, he fingered his gun.

The radio announcer first began with the local news. Anita sat motionless. Manuel wished he could see her face, but the light in the big room was too dim. He could

161

only see her silhouette as she sat, her hands gripped between her knees.

Then came the announcement he was waiting for. He stiffened, leaning forward so he could spring on Anita if she began to scream. Fuentes also moved forward.

The announcement was brief:

Pedro Certes, killer of a rent collector in Seacomb, having been shot by Detective Tom Lepski while trying to escape with three thousand dollars, has died after briefly returning to consciousness.

The announcer then began to give the racing news, but Manuel switched off. He dropped the transistor on the floor and looked hard at Anita, waiting for the first sign of hysterics.

Nothing happened.

Anita remained like a stone woman.

Except for the sound of the surf and the distant shouts of the late bathers, silence like a humid, terrible pall hung over the three in the penthouse suite.

Manuel forced himself to say, 'Dear Jesus! Anita! What can I say?'

Still she sat there, motionless.

Any moment now, Manuel thought, she will begin to scream. He got to his feet and moved towards her.

'Anita! This is a terrible thing!'

'Don't come near me!' Her voice was a harsh whisper.

Manuel paused.

The sound of her voice was so unearthly, Fuentes backed away.

A small table lamp lit up as Anita pressed the switch.

Manuel caught his breath as he looked at her face, directly lit by the lamp. He didn't recognize her. He saw before him a face that had shrivelled, aged and the eyes had retreated into their sockets.

But there was no sign of hysteria. He could be looking at the face of a dead woman.

'Anita!' He forced himself to lie. 'This is a terrible shock to me as to you.'

The dead eyes suddenly came alive.

'So you lied to me, you man of truth.' Her voice was like the rustle of dry leaves. 'You knew all the time Pedro was dying. You lied to me to unlock the doors. You lied to me so you could get your hands on all this filthy money! May God curse you!'

'Anita! No!' Manuel half shouted. 'Listen to me! I didn't lie to you! I swear it to you! Think! I am a real man of truth! I promised you your husband. When I promise one of my people something, I do everything possible to honour that promise! No, Anita, I didn't lie to you, but the man at the hospital lied to *me*! Why did he lie to me? Why did he assure me Pedro was recovering? Why?' Dramatically, Manuel banged his head with his clenched fists. 'I will find out! This I promise you! I will make him tell me why he lied, and I will punish him! This I swear to you!'

Anita closed her eyes. Tears began to run down her face.

'Pedro, my darling husband,' she moaned softly, 'I have lost you.'

Manuel gave Fuentes a quick glance. Fuentes nodded and winked. He thought Manuel's speech had been masterly.

'When we get to Havana,' Manuel said gently, 'we will arrange a Mass for Pedro. I know how you must be suffering. Cry, my poor woman. Release the agony in your heart.'

Again there was a long pause, then Anita wiped her eyes with the back of her hand and stood up.

'I will go now,' she said.

This was the last thing Manuel expected to hear. Alarmed, he stared at her.

'But, Anita, where will you go?'

'To a church. Where else? I have to light candles for Pedro. I need to pray.'

'But not now,' Manuel said in his softest tone. 'This dreadful news has shaken you. When you and I reach

Havana, we will light many candles and have a Mass said, but not now.'

She moved to the door.

'I am going.'

He moved swiftly to her, taking her arm. He felt her shiver at his touch, but he held her firmly.

'No, Anita! Think! The cops are looking for you. They will find out that it was you who unlocked the doors. You will be arrested and thrown into a cell. Think! How many candles will you light for Pedro when you are locked in a cell?'

Watching her as she stood motionless, Manuel saw a resigned, hopeless expression cross her death-like face, and he released her.

'We will go on the terrace,' he said gently. 'In the light of the moon, we will pray for the soul of your husband.' He took a furtive glance at his watch. The time was 01.05. It couldn't be long before the Warrentons returned. Somehow, he must keep this woman occupied until they did return.

Like a Zombie, Anita went with him onto the terrace. He led her to a dark corner, half hidden by a potted orange tree, its golden fruit shining in the moonlight.

They knelt side by side.

Watching, Fuentes marvelled at Manuel's hypocrisy.

* * *

In the chalet, Bradey, already made-up as a dark-skinned, youngish looking man with a chin beard and wearing a tuxedo, was working on Bannion's face.

'Your own mother won't know you by the time I've finished,' he was saying. 'If the Warrentons catch a glimpse of us before you dart them, there will be no problem. Just hold still for a moment while I fix your moustache.'

Bannion, also wearing a tuxedo, held still. He was thinking of Chrissy while Bradey worked on him. He felt

164

hollow inside. The pain-killing pills were like a comforting blanket, but he knew the teeth of this cancer was rapidly gnawing away at his vitals, like a hungry wolf tearing at the carcase of a stricken animal.

'There!' Bradey said, sitting back. 'A beautiful job. Take a look.'

With an effort, Bannion got up and surveyed himself in the bathroom mirror. He saw a big, heavily built stranger who was so unlike himself, he stared. If only he could really become this tough, strong-looking man and make himself a new life!

'Pretty good, huh?' Bradey said, grinning.

'Yes,' Bannion said quietly. 'Yes: pretty good.'

Bradey looked uneasily at him.

'Mike, you are all right?'

'I will and can do this job,' Bannion said. 'You can rely on me.' He turned and looked fixedly at Bradey. 'When this is over and I get really ill, can I rely on you to look after my daughter's interest?'

'We've gone over this before,' Bradey said. 'Relax. You will get your share in two days' time. Don't worry about it.'

Bannion took a card from his pocket.

'Lu, this is the address of the doctor who is looking after my daughter. I've talked to him on the telephone. I've told him the money will be coming.' He paused, then went on, 'Something might happen to me before I get the money. Will you take care of it for me? All you have to do is to send a money order, saying it's from me. Will you do this for me?'

Bradey felt a little chill run through him.

'But, Mike . . .'

'Don't let us discuss this further,' Bannion said curtly. 'Will you do it?'

'Of course I will.'

'Shake on it, Lu,' Bannion offered his hand.

'You think something bad will happen even in two

165

days?' Bradey asked, taking the cold, damp hand in both of his.

'I don't know. Let's call it insurance. As soon as the job is over, I'm leaving, Lu. I want to see my daughter before anything does happen. I'm not going to wait for the money. Do you mind?'

'No, of course not, Mike.'

'Thanks.'

Bradey felt himself strangely moved. He told himself if anything went wrong and there was no money, he'd damn well see this man's dotty daughter got fifty thousand dollars: no matter where it came from.

Maggie came in.

'Oh, boy! What a gorgeous meal! Now I'm all set for the house dick.' She gaped at them. 'Lu, you're a marvel. I wouldn't know either of you.'

Bradey looked at his watch.

'Let's go, Mike,' he said, then to Maggie, 'Baby, you know what to do. Keep that dick busy. When you get back here, Louis de Marney will be waiting. He's Kendrick's man. Keep him happy until we return with the loot.'

'Yes, hon,' Maggie said and kissed him.

Bradey picked up a big executive briefcase, then made for the door.

Maggie threw her arms around Bannion, giving him a kiss.

'Good luck, soldier,' she said. 'You're a lovely man!'

He smiled at her, patted her shoulder, then followed Bradey out of the chalet.

As the two men walked towards the hotel, Bannion said, 'You've got yourself a great girl, Lu.'

'A guy strikes lucky sometimes,' Bradey said. 'I guess I've struck more than lucky.'

The two men walked into the lobby. There was a scattering of the elderly still sitting around, having nightcaps. None of them paid any attention as Bradey led the way to a corner table. Two men in tuxedos were all part of the scene.

'Now, we wait,' Bradey said as they sat down. 'We look as if we're doing a deal.' He opened the briefcase and took out a sheaf of papers. Dividing the sheaf, he handed the first half to Bannion.

A waiter approached.

'Drink, Mike?'

'A coffee.'

Bradey ordered coffee and smoked salmon sandwiches. When the coffee and sandwiches arrived, he paid, tipping generously.

It was while Bradey was eating a sandwich which Bannion had refused, he saw Josh Prescott come into the lobby.

'That's the house dick,' Bradey said. 'The guy Maggie's taking care of.'

The two men watched Prescott glance around, then, leaving the hotel, he hurried towards the swimming-pool.

Then a little after 02.00, they saw the two security guards come in and speak to the night porter. They handed over keys and left.

'Going like clockwork,' Bradey murmured. 'The loot is now in the safe. We'll wait until the Warrentons arrive, then away we go.'

Ten minutes later, Maria and Wilbur Warrenton walked in. While Maria walked to the penthouse elevator, Wilbur collected the key from the night porter, than hurried after her.

Bradey stared fixedly at the diamonds as Maria waited impatiently for Wilbur to join her.

'Look at those rocks,' Bradey muttered. 'This is going to be a push over, Mike. We'll give them five minutes, then up we go, bust the safe, then by that time they should be in bed.'

Realizing that he was about to embark on his first criminal offence, Bannion felt cold sweat start out on his forehead.

His first and last, he thought, as he watched Bradey put the dummy papers into the briefcase.

Bradey looked at him.

'Okay, Mike?'

'Yes.'

They sat still, then at Bradey's nod, the two men got up and walked towards the elevator.

The night porter, busy with the breakfast list, didn't look their way.

As the elevator took them to the top floor, Bradey patted Bannion's arm.

'Going like a dream,' he said.

Eight

Rubbing his aching knees, Manuel came in from the terrace of the penthouse. He had been kneeling by Anita's side on the marble floor of the terrace, pretending to pray. He had remained on his knees, his head bowed for fifteen minutes, then unable to contain his impatience any longer, he looked furtively at her, then seeing she remained motionless, her head in her hands, he got silently to his feet, backed away, still watching her. She still remained motionless. Then he walked to the penthouse living-room.

Fuentes was sitting in a lounging chair, a cigarette dangling from his thick lips, his fat face glistening with sweat.

The two men looked at each other.

'All goes well,' Manuel said quietly. 'No hysterics. She is praying.'

Fuentes sneered.

'At a death, women always pray. What good does it do?'

'Prayer keeps them quiet,' Manuel said and smiled. 'We will have no more trouble with her.' He looked at his watch. The time was now 02.05. 'The Warrentons will be coming any time now. You take care of the man. I will take care of the woman. She might scream. Women are unpredictable. I will see she doesn't. You won't have any trouble with the man.'

Fuentes nodded, but he was thinking of Anita. She

frightened him. Hadn't she cursed him? He knew she blamed him for Pedro's death. 'Anita could be dangerous. She could spoil our plans.'

Manuel moved to the terrace doors and looked out onto the moonlit terrace. He could just see Anita, half hidden by the orange tree, still on her knees.

He turned.

'Relax, my friend. What could she do? She has no gun. She is still praying, and when women pray for their dead, they pray a long, long time.'

He would have been startled and alarmed to have known that Anita was not praying. The shock of hearing that Pedro was dead had numbed her. She had gone like a Zombie with Manuel to this dark corner of the terrace. She had knelt because he had knelt. She had closed her eyes, clasping her hands, but the prayers she had so often said were sheets of blank paper in her mind. She could only think of her husband. She saw him in a hospital bed with some hard-faced cop, sitting by his side.

Pedro Certes, killer of a rent collector in Seacomb, having been shot by Detective Tom Lepski while trying to escape with three thousand dollars, died after briefly gaining consciousness.

The words of the radio announcer burned into her brain. Pedro had died after briefly gaining consciousness! He had had no priest to comfort him and to make his peace with God. Pedro! The man she loved more than life! She thought of the months when Pedro, out of work, had relied on her to feed him, wash his clothes, pay the rent and give him what was left over of her earnings joyfully and willingly because she loved and adored him. She thought of the very few good nights when Pedro took her to some little restaurant: very few nights but which were treasured. She thought of his father's sugar cane farm. The long hours when they slaved in the burning sun. Then she was really happy, but not Pedro. He wanted to get away from the toil. He had persuaded her to go with him to Paradise City. She had been lucky to have got the part-time job of cleaning at the Spanish Bay Hotel. Pedro had assured her that soon he would find a good job. He would make a lot of money, but dear Pedro was unlucky. There was no job and no money, except what she earned.

She thought of that awful moment when Pedro had shown her a gun, and when he had told her his good friend, Fuentes, and he would make a lot of money.

Fuentes!

She thought that if it was not for this swine of a man, her dear Pedro would still be alive.

Fuentes!

That mindless brute who had tempted Pedro! That brute who had given Pedro the gun! That brute directly responsible for Pedro's death!

Anita felt a sudden rush of hot blood to her head that made her feel faint. She pressed her fingers to her temples. The faint feeling frightened her. Then the hot blood turned cold making her shudder.

She was not to know this, but, in her intensity and fury, she had suffered a rupture of a tiny blood vessel in her brain. This rupture moved her into the twilight of insanity.

Kneeling motionless, she suddenly heard a voice inside her head telling her distinctly that Pedro was crying out for revenge. The whispering voice told her that her beloved Pedro could never rest in peace until he had been revenged.

Anita, listening to this insidious voice, nodded.

'I will revenge you, darling Pedro,' she murmured. 'First, Fuentes who is responsible for your death, then Manuel who has lied to me, then this detective who shot you. They will all be punished. This, I swear to you.'

Now, she began to relax. She found she was able to pray. As she prayed, her fingers caressed the shaft of the knife concealed under her black sweat shirt as the fingers of a nun would caress her rosary.

Moving silently, his sweat-beaded bald head glistening in the moonlight, Manuel crept out on the terrace. He moved forward until he could see Anita, half concealed behind the orange tree. He watched her for a long moment, then satisfied she was still praying, he returned to the living-room.

'She is still at it,' he said. 'There will be no trouble.'

'Look!' Fuentes exclaimed, and pointed to the elevator door. The sign *Occupied* had lit up.

'Now!' Manuel smiled viciously. 'The woman will come out first. I will handle her. You point the gun at the man, and remember, no shooting.'

In the private elevator that rose from the hotel lobby up to the living-room of the penthouse, Maria Warrenton was in a gay mood. She had won twenty thousand dollars at the Casino.

'You see?' she said, giving Wilbur a kiss. 'I told you I was in a winning streak. Let's have champagne and caviar sandwiches. The excitement has made me hungry.'

Longing to go to bed and sleep, Wilbur forced a smile.

'If that's what you want, that's what you'll have,' he said and as the elevator came to rest, he pushed open the door, standing aside to let Maria pass him.

She walked into the living-room, then came to an abrupt stop as a thick arm encircled her throat and she felt a painful prick against her cheek.

'Scream, lady, and I'll slash you.' A deep, threatening voice growled in her ear.

The smell of body dirt and male sweat made her cringe. For a moment, she was paralysed with shock, but there was steel in her.

'Get away from me!' she said in a low, hard voice. 'You stink!'

Wilbur found himself facing a short, fat man wearing a soiled white shirt and tattered jeans. In his right hand, he held a revolver.

Wilbur's army training helped to absorb the shock, but looking at the enormous, vicious ape of a man holding his wife, his heart began to pound.

'Do you hear?' Maria said, still keeping her voice low. 'Get away from me!'

Manuel released her and stepped back, smiling.

'Don't let there be trouble,' he said, and waved a glittering stiletto knife. 'No one wants to get slashed. Just take it easy. Sit down, both of you.'

Maria looked at Wilbur and shrugged.

'A hold-up I suppose.' She went to the settee and sat down. 'What a bore!'

Marvelling at her courage and steady nerves, urged on by Fuentes, Wilbur went and sat by her side.

'Take the money,' Maria said contemptuously, 'and go away. You two stink.' She tossed her handbag at Manuel's feet. He kicked it towards Fuentes who picked it up, opened the bag and gaped at the pile of money Maria had won at the Casino.

'Look!' he said to Manuel. 'Look!'

Manuel paid no attention. He was staring evilly at Maria.

'Yes, lady,' he said. 'We stink because we are poor. We are not like you. You also stink to me.' He moved forward so swiftly neither Maria nor Wilbur had time to react. The glittering blade of the stiletto seemed to brush across Maria's dress. The razor-sharp blade cut across the shoulder straps. The front of the dress fell into Maria's lap.

Maria stared at her ruined dress, then up at Manuel.

'You bastard!' she exclaimed, her eyes flashing.

'Yes, lady,' Manuel again smiled evilly. 'Okay, so I'm a bastard, but you are lucky. Instead of cutting your pretty dress, I could have cut your pretty face. I could have cut off the tip of your pretty nose. So you're lucky.' He moved forward. 'So from right now, lady, you keep your mouth shut. One more word out of you and you'll lose your pretty looks.'

Maria's beauty meant more to her than anything else in the world. She turned cold. Courage oozed out of her. She grabbed hold of Wilbur's hand.

Wilbur, aware that Fuentes was standing behind him,

gun in hand, controlled his urge to spring at Manuel. This bald, bearded ape of a man chilled him. Looking at the evil smile, he was sure this man would disfigure Maria, given the slightest excuse.

Speaking hastily, he said, 'Maria, they are here for the diamonds. Take them off and drop them on the floor. Then they will go away.'

With trembling fingers, Maria reached for her earrings, but Manuel shook his head.

'No, lady, keep your pretty diamonds. What would a poor, stinking Cuban like me do with diamonds?' He shifted his stare to Wilbur. 'We want money, Mr. Warrenton! We want five million dollars! We don't leave here until we get this money in one hundred dollar bills!'

Wilbur stared at him.

'We haven't that amount of money. Take the diamonds and go!'

Again Manuel smiled evilly.

'Your pa has. We'll wait. Call him. Tell him unless we get five million dollars in one hundred dollar bills, I will cut your goddamn ears off and I'll slice your wife's face to pieces!'

Standing in the shadows, Anita listened, her fingers still caressing the haft of her knife.

* * *

In the safe room, with the safe door now open, Bradey was unlocking the security boxes. He worked with speed and dexterity, whistling *Love Is The Sweetest Thing*, his favourite theme song when he was working. As he opened each box, he handed it to Bannion who emptied the contents into the brief case.

After opening fifteen boxes, Bradey paused and flexed his fingers. He grinned at Bannion.

'Like a dream!' he said softly. 'Boy! This is better than picking apples.'

Bannion was aware of a far away stabbing pain. He was tense. Sweat beaded his face, but he managed a smile.

Bradey turned back to open more security boxes.

Thirty minutes, after the two men had entered the safe room, all the security boxes were emptied.

'Okay,' Bradey said, having replaced the empty boxes and shutting and relocking the safe door. 'Now for the Warrenton diamonds. Leave the case here. We'll come back the same way.' He looked at his watch. The time was 02.50. 'They should be in bed. Gun okay, Mike?'

'Yes.'

'Then let's go.'

Bradey pulled down the ladder that would take them to the roof.

'I'll go first.'

Silently, he climbed the ladder, pushed open the trap door and emerged out onto the roof, overlooking the penthouse terrace. Bannion, breathing heavily, forced himself to climb the ladder. The two men stood in the semi-darkness, looking down at the lighted terrace, Bradey stiffened when he saw the living-room lights were on.

'Hold it!' he whispered. 'They're not in bed yet.'

His whisper in the stillness and silence of the night carried to Anita who was standing in the shadows by the terrace door. With the swiftness of a lizard, she hid herself behind a big potted flowering shrub, kneeling down and staring up at the terrace roof. She saw two men, lit by the moonlight: the light reflected on their white shirts.

Bradey surveyed the dimly lit terrace.

'Okay, Mike, we can't waste time. Let's see what's going on.' Silently, he lowered himself from the roof to the terrace, followed by Bannion.

Bradey motioned Bannion to remain where he was, then he silently moved to the entrance to the living-room. Anita, crouching further into the shadows, watched him as he passed her within touching distance.

He peered into the lighted living-room, then he stiffened. He saw the back of a shabbily dressed man. He saw the back of the heads of Maria and Wilbur, sitting on the settee. He saw a powerfully built, bald and bearded man with a glittering stiletto knife in his hand, facing them.

In the quiet of the night, he heard this bearded man say, 'So, Mr. Warrenton, you call your pa. Tell him to bring five million dollars in cash.' The deep voice rose a note. 'You hear me?'

Bradey understood the situation immediately. The Warrentons were being held to ransom. Shifting his gaze to a big mirror across the room, he could see the Warrentons, sitting side by side: a frontal exposure. He saw the woman was wearing her fabulous diamonds. He had to restrain himself from whistling *Love is the Sweetest Thing*. This was going to be a push-over. He turned his head and beckoned to Bannion who came silently and joined him.

'Take the fat one first,' Bradey murmured. 'Then the bald guy.' His voice was just a whisper against Bannion's ear. 'Then the other two. Fast shooting, Mike.'

Bannion drew the powerful air pistol from its holster. Still keeping in the shadows, holding the gun in both hands, his arms extended, his body in a crouch, he aimed at the back of Fuentes' fat neck.

Wilbur was saying, 'I can't call my father at this hour.'

Bannion squeezed the trigger. Wilbur's voice drowned the faint plop of the gun.

Fuentes started, then rubbed the back of his neck.

'Goddamn mosquito,' he muttered.

'Call him!' Manuel barked as Bannion took aim and again squeezed the trigger. The tiny dart hit Manuel in the centre of his forehead. 'Hear me! Call him right now!' He rubbed his forehead thinking, as Fuentes had thought, that he had been bitten by a mosquito.

Shifting his aim, Bannion shot the third dart into the back of Maria's neck, then again shifting his aim, shot the fourth dart into the back of Wilbur's neck. Both of them reacted, clapping their hands to their necks.

Manuel's eyes widened as he saw Fuentes drop his gun, clutch hold of the back of the settee, then slide out of sight. Then he too felt consciousness leaving him. He took two staggering steps forward, then like a felled tree, he smashed down on an occasional table, and spread out on the floor.

Wilbur and Maria also succumbed to the powerful drug and went limp on the settee.

'Very nice,' Bradey said. 'Beautiful shooting, Mike.'

Waving to Bannion to remain where he was, Bradey moved into the living-room. Swiftly, he removed the ear-rings, the collar and the two bracelets. He dropped them into a wash leather bag which he put in his pocket.

'Come on, Mike,' he said, running out onto the terrace. 'Let's go. As I told you: smooth as cream.'

The two men hoisted themselves up onto the roof and down into the safe room.

Fifteen minutes later, the contents of the security boxes and the Warrenton diamonds were on their way to Claude Kendrick.

Bannion had removed his disguise and had changed into his chauffeur's uniform. Maggie lay on the settee, her eyes closed, moaning softly to herself. Bradey, paying her no attention, put a call through to Haddon who was waiting.

'Perfect, Ed,' he said. 'Worked like a charm. No problems.'

'Well done,' Haddon said and hung up.

Bannion came into the living-room, carrying a suitcase.

'Lu, there's an early plane to Los Angeles. I must get it.' His white face and sunken eyes told their story. 'I can't wait. Okay?'

'Sure,' Bradey said, 'The porter will get you a taxi.' He went to Bannion. 'Don't worry, Mike. You've done a swell job. The money will go to the doctor. You have my word.'

The two men shook hands, then Bradey called the night porter for a taxi.

Maggie sat up.

'You're going to see Chrissy, Mike?'

'Yes.'

'We'll miss you.' She slid off the settee and kissed him. 'Keep in touch, Lu, give him our telephone number.'

Bradey shook his head.

'No.' If something happened to Bannion and the telephone number was found on him it could lead to trouble.

Bannion understood.

'That's okay,' he said. 'It's better this way.' He heard the sound of the approaching taxi. 'I'll get off.' He looked at Bradey. ''Bye and so long.' He gave Maggie a gentle pat on her shoulder. 'It's been great knowing you,' he said, then nodding to Bradey, he left the chalet.

They listened to the sound of the taxi as it drove away.

'Is something wrong?' Maggie asked. 'He looked so sad.'

'Let's get some sleep,' Bradey said curtly. 'Come on, Maggie! I'm tired if you're not.'

'But, Lu, for him to go off like that! He looks so ill. There is something wrong, isn't there?'

Bradey put his arm around her and moved her towards the bedroom.

'He's worried about his daughter. Everyone these days has worries. Let's get some sleep. I'm tired.'

'You're tired!' Maggie snorted. 'That guy was like a sex-starved bull! Tired? I'm dead!'

* * *

From the terrace, Anita moved like a phantom to the doors of the penthouse living-room. There she paused and looked at the bodies of Manuel and Fuentes lying as

178

if dead. She looked at the inert bodies of the Warrentons on the settee.

She had watched Bradey and Bannion climb up on the penthouse roof and disappear. She had watched Bannion using some kind of gun that was practically noiseless, and here was the result!

Cautiously, she entered the living-room. On the floor by Fuentes, was a revolver. She snatched it up and backed away.

Her unhinged mind worked slowly. It was more than five minutes before she accepted the fact that these two men who had brought disaster into her life, lay at her mercy. She approached Fuentes and kicked him savagely in the face. When he didn't react, she became relaxed, and a cruel, crazy smile lit up her face. She put down the gun and fingered the haft of her knife. A murderous surge ran through her to cut this man who had tempted Pedro: cut him to pieces. Then she paused and surveyed this *de luxe* room and at the lush carpet she had cleaned so many times. It was a beautiful carpet. How often, when she had been using a vacuum cleaner, had she wished to own such a carpet!

She put the knife back into its sheaf, then catching hold of Fuentes' ankles, she dragged him out onto the terrace. She left him lying in a patch of moonlight and returned to the living-room.

She stood over Manuel, staring down at him. Had he lied to her? She felt sure he had, but, after his dramatic speech that his friend at the hospital had lied to him, she was unsure.

Then she remembered the device that would explode the bombs. Kneeling, she searched Manuel's pockets. No device, so he had lied to her!

She had a struggle to move Manuel's great body, but determination lent her strength. She was panting by the time she got Manuel lying by Fuentes' side.

179

She stood over the two men, lying unconscious at her feet.

'Pedro, try to listen to me,' she said softly. 'You are now going to be revenged. You will now be able to sleep in peace. Wherever you are, I pray you will see what your wife who has never ceased to love you, will now do to these two animals as you would want me to do to them.'

She drew the knife and knelt by Manuel's inert body. She looked with loathing at the bearded face.

'You claim to be a man of truth,' she said softly. 'All our people trusted you. You promised me my husband. You lied about the bombs. You have no machine with you to explode the bombs. You persuaded me to take great risks to hide these so-called bombs. You didn't care! All you thought about was money, you man of truth.'

On the dark horizon, a glimmer of light began to show. The sun was beginning to rise. In an hour or so, it would be dawn.

'So I punish you, you man of untruth,' Anita whispered. She thumbed back Manuel's eyelid. Her hand steady, she gently inserted the point of her knife into Manuel's retina and turned the knife gently. Leaning over him, she did the same to his left eye.

'Sightless, man of untruth, no one will come to you. No one will be betrayed by you as you have betrayed me. Live in your misery.'

As blood began to ooze out of Manuel's eyes, she got to her feet and knelt by Fuentes.

'If it wasn't for you,' she said, her voice harsh, 'Pedro would be alive now.'

Holding the haft of the knife in both hands, she began to hack and stab the unconscious body with maniacal fury.

The first rays of the sun began to light up the sky when she walked into the living-room. She went into Wilbur's bathroom and washed the blood off her hands. She then washed the knife.

She felt calmer, but not satisfied.

Pedro could still not rest in peace until this detective who had shot him was dead. She paused to think. What was his name? For a long moment, she was frightened she had forgotten, then the name came clearly to her: Tom Lepski.

But where was he? How could she find him? She didn't even know what he looked like! She thought again, then going into the living-room, she found the local telephone book.

It took her only a few minutes to locate Lepski's home address.

Again, she paused to think. This detective wouldn't be an easy target as Manuel and Fuentes. It would be dangerous to get close to him and use her knife. She ran to where she had left Fuentes' gun. Snatching it up, she left the penthouse and ran silently down the service stairs, down to the staff entrance, and out into the dawn of yet another hot, humid day.

* * *

At 07.30, Lepski was beginning his breakfast of three fried eggs and a quarter-inch thick ham, grilled crisp. Carroll sat opposite him and watched him munch with growing envy.

Carroll was a weight-watcher, and only allowed herself a cup of sugarless coffee for breakfast, but this morning, watching Lepski eat, she felt gnawing pangs of hunger. Being a woman of considerable will-power, she resisted the violent temptation of snatching Lepski's plate away and finishing up the ham and the remaining egg. However, she could not resist expressing her criticism.

'Lepski! You eat too much!' she said as Lepski speared his third egg.

'Yeah,' Lepski said. 'This is a great bit of ham.'

181

'You're not listening! You don't need such a heavy breakfast. Look at me! I only drink coffee without sugar!'

Lepski added more sugar to his coffee, then cut another piece of ham, then reached for another piece of toast.

'I've got to have a good start for the day.' He conveyed the food into his mouth and munched. 'After all, baby, I have a heavy day's work. I've got to keep my strength up.'

'You? Work! Let me tell you, Lepski, I know how you work! Most of the days you're sitting with your feet on your desk, reading the comics. When you're not doing that, you're propping up a bar making out you are a hot-shot detective. Work! You don't know the meaning of work. What about me? Me, who cleans the house, cooks your meals, washes your shirts? Me!'

Lepski had heard all this before. He gave her his oily smile.

'You're right, baby. I wouldn't know what I would do without you.'

Carroll snorted.

'All men say that!' she snapped. 'It doesn't fool any of us. From now on for the sake of your health, you will only have one egg and a morsel of ham. You'll feel and look better for it.'

Lepski widened his oily smile.

'No, baby, I've a better idea. You have one egg and a morsel of ham and I'll have my usual breakfast.'

Carroll was about to clash horns when the front door bell rang.

'Now, who can that be?' she said, pushing back her chair.

Lepski grabbed another piece of toast.

'Go ahead, baby, satisfy your curiosity,' he said, slapping butter on the toast.

'Why don't you go?' Carroll demanded. 'Do I have to do everything in this house?'

'Could be the mail man, baby, with a big, fat present for you,' Lepski said, slapping marmalade on his toast.

With an exasperated sigh, Carroll got up, walked down the passage and jerked open the front door.

To her startled surprise, she found herself confronted by a short, squat Cuban woman, dressed in black slacks and a black sweat shirt.

'Yes?' Carroll said. 'What is it?'

'I want to speak to Mr. Lepski,' Anita said. Her right hand, hidden behind her back, gripped the .38 revolver that Fuentes had dropped.

'My husband is having breakfast,' Carroll said stiffly. 'He doesn't like to be disturbed. Who are you?'

Anita regarded this good-looking woman, standing before her. Into her unhinged mind, she wondered if this woman would suffer, as she was suffering, to lose her husband.

'I am Anita Certes,' she said. 'Mr. Lepski wants to talk to me about my husband.'

'You should have gone to the station house,' Carroll said. 'Stay here. I'll ask him.'

Lepski had wiped his plate clean. He was finishing his third cup of coffee when Carroll came into the living-room.

'There's a Cuban woman,' Carroll said. 'She wants to talk to you. Her name is Anite Certes.'

Lepski sprang up, kicking his chair away.

'For the love of Mike!' he exploded. 'We've been hunting for this woman!'

Pushing Carroll aside, he stormed down the corridor to face Anita who was standing motionless.

'Are you Tom Lepski?' she asked.

A sudden feeling of chill ran through Lepski as he looked into the black, stony eyes. From experience, he knew when someone was dangerous and this woman was. He realized that his gun was in the bedroom.

'Are you the man who shot my husband?' Anita asked.

'Let's talk about it, huh?' Lepski said, gently. He realized this woman facing him, by her expression and by her wild eyes was out of her mind. 'Come on in.'

Then he saw the gun in Anita's hand, pointing at him.

Carroll, standing behind him, also saw the gun.

'Die then,' Anita said softly and pulled the trigger.

Lepski felt a thump against his heart. He started back, caught his heel on the carpet and fell heavily. His head slammed against the floor.

Anita stood over him and fired three more shots, then she turned and ran down the path and onto the street.

She wasn't to know that the gun Manuel had given Fuentes had been loaded with blanks. Manuel had distrusted Fuentes as Fuentes had distrusted him.

Seeing Lepski spread out on the floor, hearing the bang of gun fire, Carroll closed her eyes. She wasn't the fainting type. For a long moment, she remained motionless, then pulling herself together, she moved forward and knelt by Lepski's side.

This awful woman had killed him!

Cradling his head in her arms, she began to kiss him.

Lepski stirred, then his arms went around her.

'More,' he said. 'Much more.'

Carroll released him.

'I thought you were dead.'

'I thought so too.' Lepski sat up and began to rub the back of his head. 'Am I dead?'

Carroll looked at his shirt.

'There's no blood. Don't talk stupid. Of course, you're not dead!'

A little fearfully, Lepski surveyed his shirt front that showed black powder burns. Then he opened his shirt and surveyed his chest. Then with a snarl, he jumped to his feet.

'Which way did she go?' he bawled.

184

'How do I know? Oh, Tom, my love, I really thought you were dead.'

'That makes two of us.' Lepski rushed into the bedroom, grabbed up his revolver and snapped it in his holster to his belt, then he rushed back down the corridor.

Carroll caught hold of his arm as he headed for the street.

'Don't go out there! She's dangerous! No, Tom! Please!'

Lepski disentangled his arm.

'Baby, this is police work,' he said with a heroic smile that was just short of being corny. 'Look, call Beigler. Get the boys down here. Okay?'

'Oh, Tom! If anything should happen to you!' There were tears in Carroll's eyes.

Lepski loved it. He kissed her.

'Three eggs tomorrow?'

'Four if you want them. Do be careful!'

'Call Beigler.' Then bracing himself, Lepski, his hand on his gun butt, strode down the short drive onto the deserted street. Here he paused and looked to right and left. This crazy woman could not have gone far, but in which direction? Then at the far end of the street he saw Ted, the newspaper delivery boy, approaching, tossing the papers onto people's porches.

Lepski ran towards him.

'Hi, Ted!' he bawled.

The boy, thin, tall with a perpetually open mouth, gaped, then waved and came towards Lepski, peddling his bike furiously.

Lepski knew this boy was not only simple-minded, but more than retarded. He knew this boy worshipped him. Ted had told him his greatest ambition was to be as fine a cop as Lepski. Although flattered, Lepski decided that Ted's ambition was geared a lot too high.

'Hi, Mr. Lepski,' Ted said, coming to rest by Lepski's side. 'How's crime?'

Lepski knew to get the best out of Ted, he must not fluster him.

'Well, you know, Ted: they come and they go.'

Ted considered this remark thoughtfully, then he nodded.

'You're dead right, Mr. Lepski. They sure come and they sure go.' He eyed the gun on Lepski's hip. 'You ever shoot anyone with that rod, Mr. Lepski?'

'Look, Ted, did you see a woman, dressed in black coming your way?'

'I bet you have shot all kinds of thugs with that gun,' Ted said wistfully. 'One of these days, I'm going to be a cop and I'll shoot thugs too.'

Lepski contained his impatience with an effort.

'Sure, Ted, but did you see a woman, dressed in black on the street just now?'

The boy dragged his eyes away from Lepski's gun.

'A woman?' he asked.

Lepski shuffled his feet.

'A woman in black.'

'Why sure, Mr. Lepski. I saw her.'

'Where did she go?'

'Go?'

'That's right,' Lepski said, his blood pressure rising. 'Which way did she go?'

'Why I guess she went into the church.' The boy thought, then shrugged. 'You ever know anyone who would *run* to church. My Ma has to drag me to church.'

At the far end of the street was the Church of St. Mary. As Lepski began to run towards it a patrol car arrived. Two uniformed men spilled out while Ted stared, fascinated.

'The church!' Lepski snapped. 'Watch it! She's got a gun!'

Leading the way, Lepski walked down the long street, followed by the two cops who had drawn their guns.

They were immediately noticed by the neighbours who saw them from their windows, and people came out of their houses as another patrol car arrived. Then a police car came hurtling down the street to pull up with a squeal of burning tyres and Max Jacoby jumped out with two other plain-clothes detectives.

Lepski, now the centre of all eyes, paused. Ever since he had lived on this street, he had heard his neighbours say to Carroll that he was the best and most efficient detective on the force. Now was the time to hammer that praise home!

'What the hell's going on?' Jacoby demanded.

'Anita Certes,' Lepski said. 'She's out of her mind. She tried to kill me, but I guess the gun was loaded with blanks. She's in the church.'

'Well, okay, let's go get her,' Jacoby said, pulling his gun.

The group of men, guns in hand, converged on the church. The doors stood open. From the church came the smell of incense.

Lepski, with Jacoby close behind him, moved cautiously into the church, then paused.

At the far end of the aisle of the church were brightly burning candles. The altar was lit by flickering candle flames.

Lepski moved forward, then stopped.

Lying before the altar, he could see the Cuban woman. Blood was trickling down the steps of the altar. The haft of a knife grew out of her heart.

* * *

Wilbur Warrenton came slowly awake. He stared around the *de luxe* living-room, shook his head, then snapped upright. He looked at his wife by his side. She too was moving. He touched her arm gently, and her eyes opened. They looked at each other.

'What happened?' Maria asked. 'Have they gone?'

She sat up as Wilbur hauled himself unsteadily to his feet.

'We must have been drugged.' He looked around the living-room. 'Yes, I think they have gone.'

'Drugged?' Maria stared at him. 'How could we have been drugged?'

'What other explanation? Anyway, they have gone. There's no one here.'

'It's like a nightmare.' Maria stroked her throat, then she let out a faint scream. 'God! The bastards have taken my diamonds.' She jumped to her feet and would have fallen if Wilbur hadn't steadied her. 'My lovely diamonds! They've gone!'

'Maria!' Wilbur said sharply. 'Don't get hysterical. Sit down!'

'My diamonds! What will father say? They cost ten million! The bastards! I've lost my diamonds!' Maria's voice rose to a shrill screech.

'You haven't lost them,' Wilbur said. 'Stop this nonsense!'

Maria flared at him.

'How dare you talk like that to me!'

'You have not lost your diamonds,' Wilbur said, quietly and firmly.

They stared at each other, then Maria said unsteadily, 'Then where are they?'

'Where else? In the safe.'

'Am I crazy or are you? How can they be in the safe?'

'Maria, you were wearing the replicas. I promised your father that if you insisted on wearing the diamonds out of security, I was to give you the replicas to wear.'

'Replicas! I don't know what you are talking about!'

'When your father gave you the diamonds, he took me aside and gave me replicas which he had had made in Hong Kong. There, he told me, experts can convert glass into deceptive-looking diamonds. The collar, the ear-rings and the bracelets these thugs stole are made of glass.'

'God! I can't believe it!'

Wilbur went to the hidden safe, opened it and took out the leather case. He opened it and handed it to Maria who stared down at her beautiful diamonds, flashing in the sunlight.

'Oh, darling!' She put down the case, then rushed to Wilbur and hugged him. 'Thank you! Forgive me for being such a bitch. I know I am. Please help me not to be.'

Wilbur kissed her.

'Go and lie down. I have to get the police up here.'

'Lie down? I want champagne and caviar sandwiches! We must celebrate!' Maria whirled around. 'Look at the sun! Look at the sky!'

Wilbur gave a resigned shrug. He went over to the telephone to call the police. He smiled as he watched Maria walk out onto the terrace where the ultimate horror of two mutilated men was there to greet her.

THE END

GET A LOAD OF THIS

BY JAMES HADLEY CHASE

The sleazy jungle of lamp-lit streets, faded hotel lobbies and soulless freeways is the setting for a menagerie of typically brash Hadley Chase characters: all-metal blondes that weaken the resistance, merciless thugs and third-rate double-crossers, in this collection of hard-boiled stories by the thriller master, first published more than forty years ago and now appearing in paperback for the first time.

Fast-paced and crackling with wit, this classic anthology shows why James Hadley Chase is the unchallenged British champion of the tough American tradition.

0 552 13428 7

WILD TOWN

BY JIM THOMPSON

'My favourite crime novelist – often imitated but never duplicated – is Jim Thompson'
Stephen King

When David 'Bugs' McKenna is hired as the house detective for his hotel by Mike Hanlon, the town's crippled millionaire, McKenna has hopes that he can leave his violent past behind. But the death of Dudley, the hotel auditor, the disappearance of $5,000 and the unwanted attentions of Lou Ford, the town's deputy sheriff, and Joyce, Hanlon's beautiful, young wife, mean that McKenna is looking at more trouble than he can handle. And either a long, long stretch in the State Pen or a longer stay in the town cemetery . . .

'A blisteringly imaginative crime novelist . . . mesmeric abilities as a story teller . . . he outwrote James M. Cain at his most violent, amoral, terse and fast-moving . . . a classic American writer'
Kirkus Reviews

'Dashiell Hammett, Horace McCoy and Raymond Chandler . . . none of these men ever wrote a book within miles of Thompson's'
R.V. Cassil

0 552 13257 8

A SELECTED LIST OF CRIME NOVELS
AVAILABLE FROM CORGI BOOKS

☐	12792 2	The Complete Steel	Catherine Aird	£2.50
☐	12793 0	Henrietta Who?	Catherine Aird	£2.50
☐	13426 0	Parting Breath	Catherine Aird	£2.50
☐	13427 9	Slight Mourning	Catherine Aird	£2.50
☐	13237 3	Bodies	Robert Barnard	£2.50
☐	13368 X	Corpse in a Gilded Cage	Robert Barnard	£2.50
☐	13129 6	The Disposal of the Living	Robert Barnard	£2.50
☐	13127 X	Out of the Blackout	Robert Barnard	£2.50
☐	13364 7	Mother's Boys	Robert Barnard	£2.50
☐	13128 8	Political Suicide	Robert Barnard	£2.50
☐	11251 8	Cade	James Hadley Chase	£1.95
☐	13428 7	Get A Load Of This	James Hadley Chase	£2.50
☐	11308 5	You Must Be Kidding	James Hadley Chase	£2.50
☐	13350 7	The Getaway	Jim Thompson	£2.99
☐	13239 X	The Kill Off	Jim Thompson	£2.99
☐	13241 1	King Blood	Jim Thompson	£2.99
☐	13258 6	The Rip-Off	Jim Thompson	£2.99
☐	13257 8	Wild Town	Jim Thompson	£2.99